BEHOLD THE APE

JAMES MORROW

BEHOLD THE APE
Copyright © 2023 James Morrow

All rights reserved. No part of this book may be reproduced or transmitted in any form or by any electronic or mechanical means, including photocopying, recording or by any information storage and retrieval system, without the express written permission of the copyright holder, except where permitted by law. This novel is a work of fiction. Names, characters, places and incidents are either the product of the author's imagination, or, if real, used fictitiously.

The ebook edition of this book is licensed for your personal enjoyment only. The ebook may not be re-sold or given away to other people. If you would like to share the ebook edition with another person, please purchase an additional copy for each recipient. Thank you for respecting the hard work of this author.

Library of Congress Control Number: 2022951364

EBook ISBN: 978-1-68057-405-0
Trade Paperback ISBN: 978-1-68057-404-3
Dust Jacket Hardcover ISBN: 978-1-68057-406-7
Case Bind Hardcover ISBN: 978-1-68057-407-4

Cover design by Janet McDonald
Published by
WordFire Press, LLC
PO Box 1840
Monument CO 80132
Kevin J. Anderson & Rebecca Moesta, Publishers
WordFire Press Edition 2023

Printed in the USA
Join our WordFire Press Readers Group for
sneak previews, updates, new projects, and giveaways.
Sign up at wordfirepress.com

CONTENTS

1. The Woman of a Thousand Faces — 1
2. Adventures in the Brain Trade — 28
3. Dr. Pongowana's Forgotten Ancestors — 55
4. The Emperor of Aspiration — 86
5. Her Favorite Ape — 114

Acknowledgments — 145
About the Author — 147
If You Liked … — 149

*This celebration of public education
is dedicated to my friends*
MURRAY AND ROBERTA SUID,
*whose ingenious curriculum materials
have made life better for thousands of teachers.*

It shall be unlawful for any teacher in the Universities, Normals, or other public schools of the State of Tennessee ... to teach any theory that denies the story of the Divine Creation of Man as taught in the Bible and to teach instead that Man has descended from a lower order of animals.

John Washington Butler
The Butler Act, 1925
Tennessee House of Representatives

CHAPTER 1
THE WOMAN OF A THOUSAND FACES

Wherever you go, she is there. The famous monsters she created appear on postage stamps, T-shirts, lunch pails, beach towels, and mouse pads. The estate of the late Sonya Orlova has licensed her likeness, in all its iterations, to the makers of action figures, plastic model kits, collectible dolls, soft drink cups, and PEZ dispensers. Such is the legacy of Hollywood's premier horror movie actress of the 1930s—though Sonya herself would have told you, in her mesmerizing, waltz-tempo Slavic accent, that her proudest achievement was teaching filmgoers, without their even knowing it, a thing or two about the mystery of human origins.

Any serious student of popular culture can recite Sonya's signature roles without skipping a beat. Countess Nocturnia, who could transform even the most willful lover into a willing blood donor. Golemoiselle, wrought from sacred clay and secular hubris. The She-Wolf of Paris, who took such erotic delight in her lycanthropic condition.

And then, of course, there was Korgora, the Ape Woman, protagonist of five low-budget melodramas that prevented Sonya's adopted country from descending into barbarism—or so certain social historians are prepared to argue.

Born in Smolensk at the turn of the twentieth century, Sonya didn't understand at first why, two months after the start of the Great War, her hardworking, land-owning parents had gathered up their five children—plus heirlooms, photographs, and a satchel of silver coins—and sailed for New York City. Once they'd settled in the tenements of the Lower East Side, however, she began eavesdropping on Mamuska and Papa's late-night conversations, and she came to appreciate the wisdom of their decision.

Had the family stayed in Russia, they would almost certainly have gotten caught in the crossfire of the Bolshevik Revolution. Indeed, during the months leading up to the abdication of Tsar Nicholas II, and throughout the civil war that followed, nearly everyone her parents knew back home had been murdered outright or banished to a labor camp. Typical was the case of Mamuska's mystically inclined aunt, executed for aiding the Tsarina's debauched mentor, a notorious figure whose life inspired Sonya's last film, *Horror of Rasputin*, in which she played the mad monk's preferred companion, a gorilla.

For years she lived at home, supplementing the income from Mamuska's laundry business and Papa's bicycle repair shop by working as a taxi dancer at the Blue Moon Club on the other side of town. Her older siblings, meanwhile, were privileged to venture forth from Manhattan, Andrusha becoming an elementary-school teacher in Brooklyn, Yuri a dairy farmer in New Jersey, and Vasily a carpenter who, when not attending a small college in faraway Los Angeles, earned good money building motion-picture sets. Although Sonya envied her brothers their escape from the tenements, she was content to bide her time, fending off the advances of the Blue Moon clientele even as she charmed them into helping her master the bedeviling English language.

In the autumn of 1920 something happened that changed Sonya's life forever. She chaperoned her little sister, Tatiana, to the Bowery Nickelodeon and thus inadvertently saw her first horror movie. *Dr. Jekyll and Mr. Hyde* starred John Barrymore as a scientist who sought to liberate his inner Lucifer, plus Martha Mansfield as his lovelorn fiancée and Nita Naldi as the music hall floozy with whom Jekyll's lecherous other half carries on a lurid affair. According to the program notes, Barrymore had accomplished the first transformation without benefit of make-up, relying solely on his ability to twist his pliable face and contort his spidery body. The plot was equally enthralling, so tragic, so wrenching, so worthy of her tears: poor, deluded Henry Jekyll, thinking he could have it both ways—philanthropic physician by day, sybarite by night, blithely oblivious to the disasters he was courting.

"I could play that part," Sonya remarked after the picture as she and Tatiana sauntered through the lobby. She indicated a lithographed *Dr. Jekyll and Mr. Hyde* poster resting on an easel.

"The fiancée?" said Tatiana. "Of course! Martha Mansfield is pretty, and you're even *prettier*."

"No, not the fiancée."

"The music hall lady?"

"Not Miss Gina," said Sonya. "The monster."

"Edward Hyde?"

"Let's call her Edwina."

"What about Henry?"

"You mean Henrietta?" said Sonya. "She's a crashing bore, but I'd be willing to play her for the sake of becoming Edwina. Put me in front of a camera, and my wicked Lady Hyde will make grown men shit their pants."

"Sonya!"

Because her eldest brother was still nailing together Hollywood scenery for a living, her notion of insinuating herself into the movie business struck Sonya as only moderately preposterous, and so with her parents' reluctant blessing she traveled by train across the North American continent, bound for a city she imagined would prove as gloriously decadent as the Spitalfields district of Hyde's nocturnal ramblings.

Shortly after appropriating the spare room in the cottage her brother was renting in El Sereno, she realized she'd made a mistake, for in becoming Vasily's tenant she'd also become his captive audience. An angular, elfin man with wild eyes and untamed hair, Vasily spent his nights railing against humankind's collective stupidity and God's monolithic indifference. Depressingly for Sonya, Vasily no longer orbited the movie business, having been, as he put it, "improperly fired for allegedly drinking on the job." A year earlier, he'd managed to graduate from Occidental College, then somehow got accepted to the Pasadena School of Medicine. He'd dropped out after six months, and yet, in his gin-fueled delusions, he was convinced he'd eventually become as competent as any credentialed doctor.

"In two or three years I'll have mastered more human physiology than half the instructors at the Pasadena

School. Give me a talented amateur over an uninspired professional any day."

"But how will you acquire actual medical knowledge?" asked Sonya.

"I still have my textbooks, and I can attend the lectures at Mercy Hospital *incognito*."

"Lectures by uninspired professionals?"

"This is a brilliant plan, dear sister. Some day you'll understand."

Because Sonya's taxi-dancer experience transferred readily to Los Angeles, she eventually saved up enough to escape from Vasily's sphere. She signed a lease on a Culver City bungalow in which roaches were forever showing other roaches around the place. Despite these seedy accommodations, her spirits remained high. Before long she acquired not only a boyfriend, Homer Chilton, who wrote the popular science-fiction radio drama series *Ticket to Tomorrow* (they met standing in line to see Lon Chaney in *The Unholy Three*), but also a reasonably honest manager, Barney Garland, and eventually she broke into the business—first as an extra, then as a bit player, and finally as a name in the credits.

To whom did a casting director turn when he needed someone to essay the ingénue's simpering best friend in a cliffhanger? To Miss Orlova, of course. The French goose girl in a Great War spectacle? The callow young hero's slut-on-the-side in a domestic melodrama? The pitiable harlot in some high-minded attempt at social realism? Indeed. While this was hardly the career she'd imagined for herself after falling under John Barrymore's spell, she resolved to continue playing incarnated plot necessities, taking every opportunity to learn about those technical elements—camera angles, lenses, lighting, filters, gels—that could turn a performance into a phenomenon.

She even invested in a Max Factor make-up kit, complete with crepe wigs, false noses, spirit gum, greasepaint, and dental appliances. Every night she practiced the art of turning herself into a creature of darkness, devising her own interpretations of Gaston Leroux's sympathetic Phantom of the Opera, Aleksey Tolstoy's undead Wurdalak, Nikolai Gogol's demonic Viy, and, of course, Robert Louis Stevenson's soulless Mr. Hyde. And then, at the crack of dawn, she would dutifully report to the set, prepared to become whatever scatterbrained or promiscuous young woman was paying the rent that week.

Occasionally Sonya visited Vasily, hoping to rekindle the affection they'd known as children, but these days her brother regarded her only as a source of ready cash. Having moved to Santa Monica, he now occupied something called a Slipstream trailer, a kind of landlocked, aluminum-plated dirigible, though he was really living inside his head, a terrain of epic self-deception, or so Sonya surmised from their conversations in his kitchenette.

"My life is on track," he insisted, gesturing toward the medical textbooks stacked on the mattress. "I've read them three times over, and I've snuck into dozens of lectures, and next month I'll arrange to get listed in the *Southern California Registry of Licensed Physicians*, also the Orange

County Telephone Directory. Vasily Orlov, MD —that's me."

"The instant prospective patients see this place, they'll run screaming," said Sonya.

"Until I have my own clinic, I intend to make only house calls."

"'Look, Mildred, it's the Angel of Death, come to pay us a visit.' How much do you want this time?"

"Lend me a hundred, and I'll own the Slipstream free and clear. I'll repay you once I have three or four regular patients."

"God help them."

"I'll pretend you didn't say that."

"I'll pretend you're about to become acquainted with reality."

In 1927 Warner Bros. released, to considerable success, *The Jazz Singer*, featuring lip-synched songs and a smattering of recorded dialogue, and soon almost everyone in Tinseltown was convinced that talkies would take over the industry. At her manager's urging, Sonya queued up for a Vitaphone screen test conducted by Excelsior Pictures—not exactly a Poverty Row outfit like Mascot or Tiffany but hardly commensurate with Paramount or Metro. The audition rules allowed Sonya to use her choice of material, so she performed her version of Dr. Jekyll's chemistry experiment. Like Barrymore, she transmuted into her second self without resorting to make-up, interpolating lines such as

"You'll never control *me*, my pathetic Henrietta!" and "Lead me into temptation, my lascivious Edwina!"

Upon seeing Sonya's astounding metamorphosis, the president of Excelsior, Isaac Bachman, summoned her to his Gower Street office. "The camera likes you, darling," he gushed. "The microphone likes you *better*. The whole *meshuggener* world will *love* you. I'm sending Barney a contract tomorrow."

Playing a hunch, Mr. Bachman cast Sonya as the vampire protagonist in a horror movie he'd rushed into production with an unfinished script and an incomplete cast. His reasoning was simple. *Variety* had predicted that Universal's forthcoming supernatural fantasy, *Dracula*, starring Bela Lugosi, would strike a chord with audiences seeking a respite from the anxieties that, following the Crash of '29, had been visited upon millions of moviegoers. So why, asked Isaac, shouldn't Excelsior get there first?

"The picture's called *Countess Nocturnia: Mistress of the Dead*. You'll play a bloodsucker who's as beautiful as she is treacherous."

"Everybody in this town is beautiful," said Sonya. "I want to be *unforgettable*."

"How about beautiful *and* unforgettable?"

"Give me a weekend with my Max Factor kit, Mr. Bachman, and I'll reward you with you a Nocturnia who's gorgeous, ghastly, and dangerous to know."

Guided only by her reflection in the mirror and a handful of sketches, Sonya turned her eyes into bottomless pools of menace, worked her hair into a coiffure as unruly as Medusa's, and outfitted her upper teeth with a denture suggesting a guillotine for mice. Homer the boyfriend called her Nocturnia make-up "a glorious obscenity." Mr. Bachman took one look and cried, "It's a by-God masterpiece! *Mazel tov!*"

Countess Nocturnia beat *Dracula* into theaters by three months and did surprisingly well at the box office. Even after the Lugosi picture was released, Sonya's vampire drew enthusiastic audiences. The reviews were mixed—whereas *Daily Variety* called the film "Grand Guignol in the grand tradition," the *Los Angeles Times* lamented its "penny-dreadful sensationalism"—but the profits were undeniable. Mr. Bachman credited Grant Ferris's efficient direction and Ray Erlich's moody photography, but he reserved most of his praise for Sonya's "brilliant acting and miraculous make-up."

Unsurprisingly, he lost no time developing *Blood of Nocturnia* and commissioning scripts for more such vehicles. *She-Wolf of Paris* had Sonya essaying a dual role as *Belle Époque* explorer Françoise Vicot and her silver-furred alter ego. The picture performed so well that Mr. Bachman immediately hustled *Cry of the She-Wolf* into production. Next came *Golemoiselle: Creature of Clay*, in which Sonya played a living sculpture animated by a deranged Kabbalist. *Revenge of Golemoiselle* followed in short order.

And so it was that she stopped being an actress and became an entirely different class of person, a movie star. Wilton Crabbe at *Daily Variety* said it best. "At long last Hollywood can boast a female equivalent of the late Lon Chaney. Sonya Orlova is our Woman of a Thousand Faces."

When Vasily appeared at Excelsior one sweltering July afternoon, wending his way among the plaster tombstones on the *Kiss of Nocturnia* set, Sonya realized he was the last person she wanted to see—and yet his frightened eyes and trembling hands aroused her sisterly instincts, and so she resolved to listen to his latest tale of woe. She'd just delivered an adequate reading of "No grave this side of Perdition can hold me" to her servant, Mordant, which meant Scene 14 was in the can. Mr. Ferris ordered the cameraman to cut, the property master to kill the fog machine, and the lighting technician to douse the kliegs.

"What a *fantastic* make-up job." Vasily wore a white lab coat, as if that gave him the authority to come crashing onto Hollywood soundstages. "Of course, nothing can top your Golemoiselle. I'm *dying* to see the next sequel."

"How much this time?" she asked.

"I'm not here for money. Sonya, do you believe in sin?"

"Yes. No. I don't know. What the hell kind of question is that?"

"I believe I've committed a sin."

"For whatever reasons, Mother Church never got her hooks into me, and I wouldn't exactly call our parents religious either. Why are we having this conversation?"

"A terrible, unpardonable sin. You're the only person I can talk to."

"It will take me an hour to get this crap off my face."

"There's a bar at the corner of Sunset and Talmadge. I'll

meet you there."

By the time Sonya arrived at the Mesa Magnifica, Vasily was in his cups, contemplating an empty martini glass that could have served as a birdbath (the bar was celebrating the end of Prohibition in style). She joined him in the booth and ordered a glass of stout, the preferred beverage of Barrymore's Mr. Hyde.

"While you were on this side of town becoming a horror queen, I was also doing pretty well for myself," said Vasily. "I rented an abandoned sanitarium in Pico Rivera, converted the turret into a surgical theater—"

"So it's *surgery* now? *Surgery*?"

"Brain surgery, to be precise."

"Good God."

"I'll have you know that my assistant and I—"

"Another graduate of the Famous Surgeons Correspondence School?"

"A nursing student."

"Are you sleeping with her?"

Vasily rolled his eyes. "During the past eighteen months Nurse Cassidy and I have removed—"

"*Nurse* Cassidy? She graduated?"

"At the Orlov Clinic we don't fetishize diplomas. Our specialty is cerebral neoplasms. Thus far we've saved the lives of four Chinese laborers, but recently I've learned about the drawbacks of running a private neurosurgery practice."

"Second-degree murder?" said Sonya, wondering how she could talk herself out of turning Vasily over to the police.

"Two months ago I was offered seven thousand dollars to relocate a dead scientist's frozen disembodied brain into the skull of a gorilla."

"To do *what*?"

"Naturally I assumed the clients wanted a complete swap, one whole brain for another, but they told me to transplant the left cortical hemisphere only."

"Into a ... gorilla?"

"An eastern lowland gorilla. His name is Zolgar."

"Half a frozen human brain?"

"My clients, a textbook publisher called Nigel Rowen and his brother—they told me everybody would benefit. Without the surgery, Zolgar was doomed—a malignant brain tumor—and the operation would give the dead scientist a new lease on life."

"Why did the Rowens have a frozen human brain in the first place?"

"They wouldn't say."

"For that matter, why were they keeping a dying gorilla?"

"Seven thousand dollars, Sonya. Now I can buy the place I'm renting."

"Something tells me you weren't your clients' first choice of surgeon."

"I severed the donor's *corpus callosum* as they wished, returned his right hemisphere to the ice chest, and transplanted his left into the ape's cranium."

"And that happened to Zolgar's diseased hemisphere?"

"Nigel and Desmond didn't want it, so I disposed of it discreetly."

"Why didn't they have you insert *both* of the scientist's hemispheres and give him an *entirely* new lease on life? Were they inordinately fond of Zolgar?"

"I've asked myself those same questions."

"This is all very disturbing."

"You haven't heard the worst of it." Vasily lifted the skewered olive from his martini glass. "The Rowens demanded that during the procedure I implant an electrode in the gorilla's medulla." He closed his lips around the olive and pulled it free of the toothpick. "I suspect they're shaping his behavior through radio-controlled shocks."

"Would you mind if Homer appropriated all this for the next installment of *Ticket to Tomorrow*?"

Vasily removed a *Los Angeles Times* clipping from the inside pocket of his lab coat: a full-page, lavishly illustrated advertisement for a traveling carnival called *Pollock and Boggle's Peripatetic Panorama of Beasts, Freaks, and Prodigies*. According to the promotional copy, the carnival with its "six stupendous sideshows" would occupy the Pomona Fairgrounds "for two thrill-packed weeks only."

DARWIN'S ORIGIN OF SPECIES.

SEE Eloise the Bearded Lady!

SEE Ling and Loo the Chinese Siamese Twins!

SEE Swami Gupta the Astonishing
Hindoo Mind Reader!

SEE Zolgar the Gorilla
Who Receives Messages from Heaven!

SEE Armless Jake
Who Throws Knives with His Feet!

SEE Cornelius the Crocodile
Who Snaps Chains with His Jaws!

"The engraving of Zolgar looks like the ape I operated on, and the names match," said Vasily. "I need to get to the bottom of this."
"I don't."
"Can we drive to Pomona tonight?"
"I'm exhausted."
"A big movie star like you—you must own a car."
"A Studebaker, a hundred shares of Excelsior Pictures, and a rundown mansion in Bel Air. I'm really tired."
"Damn it, Sonya, my patient is being *exploited*."
"Here's the deal. Ferris doesn't need me on Thursday. I'll appear outside your clinic at noon, and if you're sober, we'll go visit Zolgar."
"For his sake, I'll hold up my end of the bargain."

She surveyed Zolgar's portrait. "He obviously deserves better, to say nothing of the scientist."

"Maybe you should bring your checkbook."

As Sonya had anticipated, Homer thought Vasily's foray into cross-species brain surgery might make an engaging radio drama, so he asked to join the expedition. Against all odds, it was a sober and even sedate Vasily who strode out of the former sanitarium, a brick monstrosity on Loch Lomond Drive. He approached Sonya's Studebaker at a steady gait, his breath smelling only of jelly donuts, and climbed into the back seat.

Despite Homer's incipient potbelly and pasty complexion—it was hard for a white person not to acquire a tan in Southern California, but somehow he'd managed it—Sonya found him physically attractive. Over time their relationship had achieved a congenial equilibrium. Neither partner had any use for matrimony. Both periodically required total privacy and spaces to call their own (and to mess up accordingly), hence Sonya's deed to the shabby Bel Air mansion she called Medusa Manor and Homer's long-term lease on a decrepit houseboat in Marina del Rey. They regularly visited each other's sovereign domains, sleeping in yin-yang conviviality and making breakfast together the next morning—and yet their "getaway cars," as Homer put it, her Studebaker and his Oldsmobile, remained indispensable to the arrangement.

For nearly an hour Sonya drove them east through the

suburban wasteland that stretched from LA to Pomona. Vasily spent the trip jabbering about the protocols he'd devised for managing Zolgar's case. Thanks mostly to experimental drugs, he'd minimized swelling, staved off bacterial infection, and forestalled tissue rejection. By the time they reached the fairgrounds, she found herself admitting that, as irresponsible quacks go, her brother was evidently among the best.

With its tatty attractions and bracingly sordid atmosphere, Pollock and Boggle's Peripatetic Panorama put Sonya in mind of Tod Browning's *Freaks*, the second picture he'd made after his *Dracula* success. Calliope music rode the afternoon breezes. Gamey fragrances thickened the air. A single 35-cent ticket admitted a customer to all the sideshows. Briefly the group patronized the Siamese twins, who were apparently the real thing, spliced together by a vivid fleshy seam, but they decided to pass up the bearded lady, the mind reader, the armless knife-thrower, and the steel-jawed crocodile, heading instead for the tent with the A-frame billboard touting the spiritual spectacle that lay beyond.

Sister Celeste Torrance
the Evangelical Wonder
Presents

Brother Zolgar
the Primate Prophet
Next Show 2:00 PM

The sweet scent of musty canvas permeated the interior of the tent. Sonya spotted three empty chairs in the back row. As she and her companions settled in, the other patrons released a collective gasp. Dressed in a burlap coat and worn-out sandals, Brother Zolgar crept out from behind a curtain on all fours and swayed his way toward a blackboard suspended beside a plywood pulpit. Having never seen a live ape before, Sonya was immobilized by amazement.

Now a dainty, dimpled young woman, wearing a robe of shimmering white chiffon, appeared and stood behind the pulpit. Sister Celeste Torrance beamed extravagantly while rotating her head and trunk in an arc, as if delivering a separate, personalized smile to each and every audience member.

"Ladies and gentlemen, seekers and searchers, wanderers and wayfarers," she said in a high, breathy voice, "we have among us today a citizen of the Congo who became a prophet after being visited by an angel." She sashayed up to the gorilla and presented him with a stick of chalk. "Brother Zolgar, tell us the angel's name."

The gorilla snatched the chalk away and wrote MOIRA on the blackboard in squiggly capital letters.

"Did Moira give you the power to understand human language?"

YES.

"Did she teach you how to talk?"

APE LARYNX CAN'T MAKE HUMAN SOUNDS.

A stumpish man in a pinstripe suit pushed a canvas flap aside and entered the tent holding a vacuum-tube console trailing an electric cord. Taking a seat in the third row, he balanced the device on his knees: a radio receiver, Sonya decided, though instead of a dial it had a red pushbutton.

"What did Moira tell you about the origin of your species?" asked Sister Torrance.

Zolgar began to write, but his broad shoulders obscured the audience's view. He stepped away and with an open palm gestured toward the slate.

EVOLUTION.

The pinstriped man pushed the red button. A subtle spasm passed through the gorilla, roiling his fur head to toe.

"Good Lord," muttered Homer.

Zolgar's frightened gaze shifted from the incendiary word to the radio—not a receiver after all, Sonya realized, but a transmitter—and back again. Hastily he supplemented his answer.

EVOLUTION IS AN EVIL NOTION.

Several patrons applauded.

"Tell us more," said Sister Torrance.

MY ANCESTOR WAS APE WHO LIVED WITH ADAM IN EDEN.

Approving murmurs filled the tent, though none of them came from Sonya or her companions. The sheer vulgarity of Sister Torrance's act, and the electric coercion on which it turned, set her teeth on edge.

"Does anyone have a question for Brother Zolgar?" Sister Torrance's sweeping gesture encompassed the entire audience.

A young woman in a pink blouse haltingly addressed the Primate Prophet. "Exactly ten years ago, the Scopes Trial began in Dayton, Tennessee. Do you know about it?"

As Sister Torrance cleaned the slate, Zolgar cast a wary eye on the pinstriped man.

SCOPES RIGHTLY FOUND GUILTY. TAUGHT MEN ARE MONKEYS.

"What do you say to people who believe in the Darwinian theory?" asked a strapping young man in a plaid flannel shirt.

Oddly enough, Sonya had recently heard a character in an old-house thriller, *The Monster Walks*, featuring an allegedly homicidal chimpanzee, use that very phrase, "the Darwinian theory."

LOVE GOD'S DESIGNS, NOT DARWIN'S GUESSES.

"I have truly sinned," said Vasily.

As Sonya approached the Peripatetic Panorama headquarters, a rusty trailer on the far side of the fairgrounds, she wondered whether Messrs. Pollock and Boggle knew about the implanted electrode and the pinstriped man. She liked to think they were either ignorant of the Rowen brothers' *modus operandi* or regarded it as essential to the public service Sister Torrance was providing.

Vasily rapped on the trailer door.

"Come in!" piped up a reedy male voice.

Entering, the three Panorama patrons encountered a

dwarf dressed in a tuxedo and smoking a cigarette. He greeted them with a scowl that seemed larger than his face.

"Whaddaya want?"

"We would like to see Mr. Pollock or Mr. Boggle," said Sonya.

"Lester Boggle's wife shot him last week. Didn't you read about it?"

"I hope it's not serious," said Vasily.

"His affair with the bearded lady was serious, likewise the bullet in his heart," said the dwarf. "You'll have to settle for Mr. Pollock." He turned and shouted toward the back of the trailer. "Hey, Sam! You off the can yet?"

Somebody flushed a toilet. A corpulent, broken-nosed man appeared from behind a blanket, hoisting up his trousers. Banded with saliva, a blimp of a cigar jutted from between his yellow teeth.

"Good afternoon, sir," said Sonya's brother. "I am Dr. Vasily Orlov. My colleagues and I hope you can spare a minute, as per that venerable maxim, 'The customer is always right.'"

"You want your money back?" growled Sam Pollock. "Take it up with Lester."

"I thought Mr. Boggle was dead," said Vasily.

"He is. That's what I think of your maxim."

Sonya could scarcely believe her good luck. Pollock was gripping the June issue of *Photoplay*, which included a six-page illustrated feature about the Woman of a Thousand Faces.

"That happens to be me on the cover," she said, pointing.

Pollock held the *Photoplay* cover adjacent to Sonya's face. His gaze oscillated between the full-color studio portrait of Nocturnia and the strange woman in his trailer.

"Christ, it really *is* you! I'm your biggest goddamn fan!"

"Then maybe we can do business," said Sonya. "I was enthralled by something I saw today, and I must have it."

"You're offerin' to buy my carnival?"

"Just one act."

"Call me Tyrone," said the dwarf. "Can I call you Sonya? Can I tell my kids I'm on a first-name basis with the She-Wolf of Paris?"

"Sure, Tyrone," said Sonya. "Let's all go camping sometime."

"Which act?" said Pollock.

"The Primate Prophet."

"He's not for sale. He's not even mine to sell. Your scheme's outta the question. Forget about it. Nothin' doin'. How much did you have in mind?"

"Five thousand dollars," said Sonya. "I have my checkbook with me."

"Jeepers." Pollock looked like a child who'd just inherited a candy store. "What does a movie star want with her own private revival meeting?"

"Zolgar is being treated cruelly," said Sonya.

"Here's the problem," said Pollock. "The two gentlemen who put the act together—"

"We know all about the Rowen brothers," said Vasily. "Matter of fact, I'm the surgeon who augmented their gorilla's brain."

"Is that so?" said Pollack. "The thing is, the Rowens pay me twenty bucks a week to exhibit Zolgar. They also cover Sister Torrance's salary."

"At twenty dollars a week, how long would you have to showcase Zolgar to make five thousand?" asked Sonya.

"I'm not good at arithmetic," said Pollock.

"Five years," said the dwarf, "and only if they worked every week."

"Of course, the Rowens would have me arrested if I simply went and sold their monkey," said Pollock.

"Ape," said Vasily.

"Tell 'em it ran away," Homer suggested.

"Yeah—to Tijuana," added Tyrone.

"Here's the other problem," said Pollock. "For me to simply throw Celeste out in the street would be unethical."

"As opposed to torturing a gorilla six times a day?" said Homer.

"Torturing?" said Pollock.

"You don't know about the red button?" said Homer.

"Red button?"

Sonya experienced a double revelation: Pollock was lying, and it didn't matter.

"While we're negotiating for Zolgar," said Vasily, "maybe we can reach a settlement with the young woman."

Pollock rested his hand on Tyrone's head as if he were a newel post. "Go get Celeste."

The dwarf disappeared, and for the next fifteen minutes Sonya, Homer, and Vasily listened patiently as Sam Pollock summarized the screenplay he'd written last winter, a horror melodrama about a traveling carnival in which all the performers were zombies.

"Tyrone typed it up. The carbon's around here somewhere. Would you like to see it?"

"Not just now, thanks," said Sonya.

"I've titled it *Horror Beneath the Bigtop*. Or do you prefer *Charnel House Jamboree*?"

"Go with your first instinct," said Sonya. "Nobody knows what a charnel house is."

Now the dwarf returned with the delicate Celeste, who radiated the disgruntled air of a bridesmaid who believed the groom should've been hers.

"Tyrone tells me I'm about to lose my job," she snorted. "Just so you'll know, Miss Nocturnia, if you manage to shut down my Zolgar act, the Rowens don't have any other work for me. This whole situation stinks to high heaven."

"Sister Torrance," said Vasily, "I could always use a second surgical assistant."

"Unless, of course, you've had formal medical training," said Sonya.

"You do surgery?" said Celeste.

"I'm the doctor who planted a human cerebral hemisphere in Zolgar," said Vasily. "I can start you at eighteen dollars a week."

"I convinced the Rowens I was an evangelical wonder," said Celeste. "I can probably convince your patients I'm a nurse."

"From your performance this afternoon," said Homer,

"I would've sworn you're a genuine revival-meeting queen, another Aimee Semple McPherson."

"Look around," said Celeste. "Do you think Sam's hooey show is a friggin' *church*? Tell you the truth, I'm not the world's most religious person."

"You could've fooled me," said Tyrone.

"Can you tell us why the Rowens went to all this trouble?" asked Sonya.

"They say they're defending God's honor. Of course, their *own* honor could use a bit of polishing. They stole Zolgar from a veterinary clinic in Burbank."

"*Stole* him?" said Homer. "Then they can hardly question Mr. Pollock's right to sell him."

"Sister Torrance," asked Vasily, "have you any idea who owned the human brain the Rowens brought to me?"

"I certainly do," said Celeste with a fleeting smile. "You'll never guess."

"Tell us."

"Am I definitely on your payroll?"

"You'll find the work fulfilling. At the Orlov Clinic we treat epilepsy, hydrocephaly, blastomas…"

"Where will I live?"

"I have a guest cottage," said Sonya.

"Do I gotta share it with the monkey?"

"He'll get his own suite in my mansion."

"I hate to say it, but I'm not convinced the Rowens will believe Zolgar simply hied himself to Mexico," said Pollock.

"Might I ask you a favor, Sam?" Sonya pulled her checkbook from her shoulder bag. "Would you mind if I showed *Horror Beneath the Bigtop* to Isaac Bachman at Excelsior?"

"Would I *mind*?"

"If it's half as exciting as what you've described…"

"It sounds great to me, too," said Homer, "and I'm the head writer on *Ticket to Tomorrow*."

"Did you write the one about the nine starfish who get to be an actual constellation in the sky?" said Celeste.

"Everybody's favorite," said Homer.

"But did you write it?"

"Well, no. I thought it was maudlin."

Pollack rummaged around in a steamer trunk and, retrieving the carbon copy of his script from beneath a stack of gaudy pulp magazines, placed it in Sonya's grasp. "Of *course* you can show it to Mr. Bachman."

"So we have a bargain—right?"

"Done and done," said Pollock.

Sonya deposited the carbon in her bag, wrote $5,000 on the topmost check, and recorded the date. "Do I make it out to 'Sam Pollock,' 'Peripatetic Panorama,' or what?"

"My current financial institution knows me as 'Nathan W. Treet.' That's T-r-e-e-t."

"Sam likes to move his funds around," Tyrone explained. "It simplifies matters when the bank mistakenly bounces a check."

Sonya wrote, "Nathan W. Treet," then passed the check to Pollock, who folded it in half and secured it in his wallet.

"So tell me, Sister Torrance—who was the brain donor?" asked Vasily.

"That poor dead scientist the Rowens can't stand. You know, the one with the monkey theory. The Victorian chump called Darwin."

"Charles Darwin?" said Vasily. "That's crazy."

"No," said Celeste. "That's show business."

CHAPTER 2
ADVENTURES IN THE BRAIN TRADE

Because scores of Californians had probably driven to the Pomona Fairgrounds that day just to see the Primate Prophet, Sam Pollock demanded that Celeste present all three of her remaining shows. Sonya arrived at the end of the last performance, which found Zolgar writing HE'S COMING AGAIN SOON on the blackboard. The audience released a torrent of applause.

As the pinstriped man exited the tent, clutching the transmitter, Sonya elbowed her way through the departing crowd and mounted the dais. The gorilla was now squatting beside the altar, staring into space, a study in simian despair.

"Brother Zolgar, this is Sonya Orlova," said Celeste, cleaning the slate. The gorilla lifted his head. "Sonya, meet Zolgar."

The Primate Prophet rose and shambled to the blackboard. GOOD EVENING, MISS O. RELATIVE OF DR. O?

"My brother," said Sonya.

BEHOLD THE APE   29

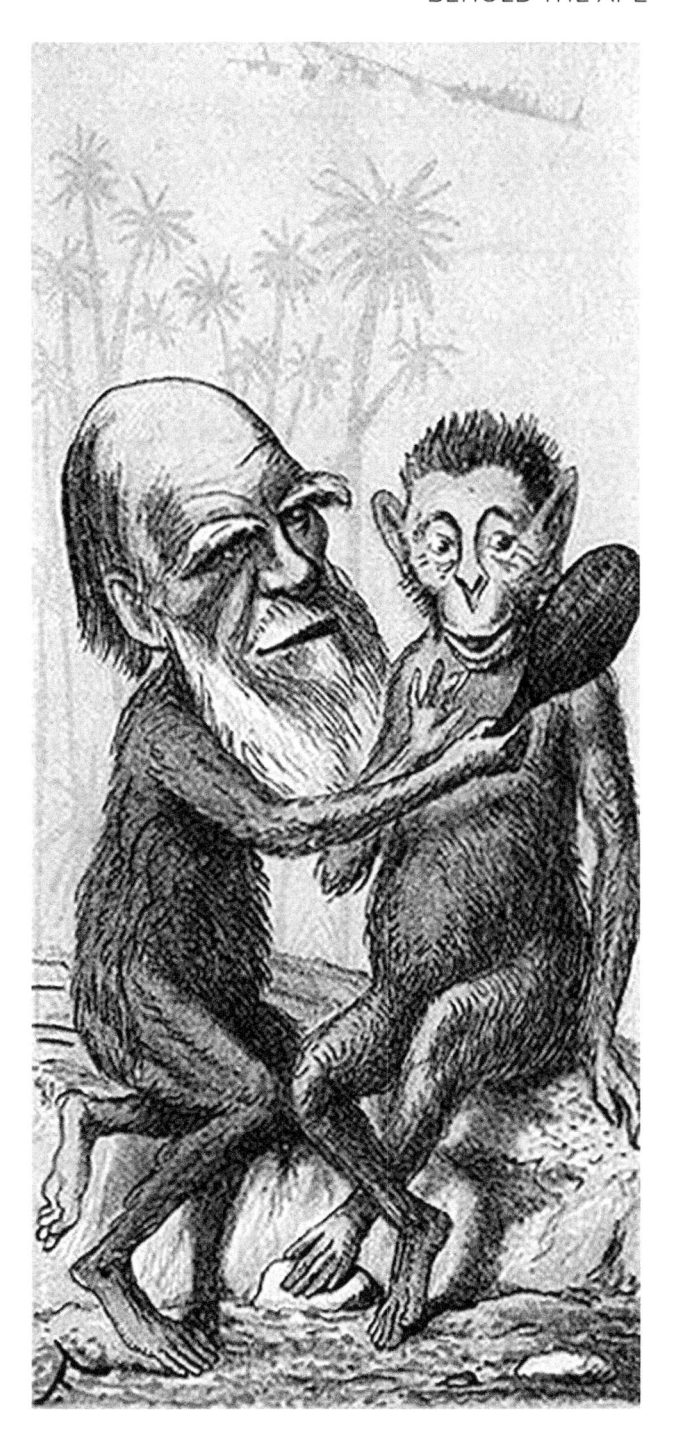

I HAVE MIXED FEELINGS ABOUT HIM.

"So do I. But it's really the Rowens who did this to you."

FRESH FRUIT?

"Sorry."

CIGARETTE?

"Alas."

Sonya approached the immense animal. His fur was redolent of silt and brine, a not unpleasant fragrance. His wide, soft eyes and dramatic nostrils appealed to her aesthetic sense, in the manner of an Expressionist painting.

"Do you prefer 'Zolgar' or 'Mr. Darwin'?"

I AM HALF OF EACH.

"I think of you as 'Mr. Darwin.' The Rowens have treated you abominably. Would you like to leave this awful sideshow and come live with me?"

For a full minute the gorilla simply stared at her, wonderstruck. Recovering his composure, he wrote, SPLENDID!

"Were you serious about the guest cottage?" asked Celeste.

"Pack your suitcase," said Sonya.

"Done already. It's one of Sam's rules. 'Always be prepared to scram on short notice. You never know when a sheriff will find fault with our fake permits.'"

Although Mr. Darwin cut a conspicuous figure as he ambled across the parking lot, sometimes walking nearly upright, more often using his arms as front legs, he attracted no particular attention. This was the Peripatetic

Panorama, after all, where the women had beards and the men were joined at the hip. The ape hoisted his hairy bulk into the back of the Studebaker, causing the chassis to tilt and the shock absorbers to squeal. The remaining space was large enough only for Celeste, which meant Homer and Vasily had to sit up front with Sonya.

The rescue party was soon speeding away from the fairgrounds through a dismal night clotted with fog and drizzle.

"He wants to write a message," Celeste announced.

Sonya told Homer to take *Horror Beneath the Bigtop* out of the glove compartment. He passed the script to the gorilla, who peeled off the first page and flipped it over. Celeste placed a pencil in his fist.

"Dr. Orlov, he says he forgives you," she reported.

"I appreciate that," said Vasily.

For the next twenty minutes, Mr. Darwin continued to write.

"He even feels *grateful* to you," Celeste told Vasily. "Back in England, he was sick all the time. Headaches, nausea, the flux. His new body is much healthier. He also forgives me. He'll never forgive the red-button man."

Sonya firmed her grip on the steering wheel. This eventful day, quite possibly the strangest of her life, could not end too soon.

After five more miles, Celeste piped up again. "He has to take a dump."

"Oh, for Christ's sake," said Sonya.

"He says it can't wait."

"There's a restaurant about a mile down the road," said Vasily. "Viva Zapata."

"Actually, I could go for some Mexican food right now," said Homer. "We'll tell 'em we spent the day shooting *Tarzan and the City of Gold*, and our star gorilla has a big appetite for burritos."

"He eats only fruits and vegetables," noted Celeste.

"Tortillas are a vegetable, I think," said Homer.

"I'm really looking forward to this," said Sonya evenly.

As it happened, Sonya's knowledge of Charles Darwin's accomplishments was not limited to minor characters expounding on "the Darwinian theory" in low-budget horror films. Shortly after landing in New York, Mamuska and Papa had decided to supplement their children's public education. When it came to science and mathematics, Mamuska convinced her erudite brother, likewise in flight from the Bolsheviks, to tutor his nieces and nephews. His most memorable lecture concerned what he called "the tree of life." According to Uncle Kostos, Charles Darwin had persuasively demonstrated that all living things, past, present, and future, were bound together in a single tapestry of vast scope, overwhelming variety, and endless complexity.

"We immigrants can especially appreciate Darwin's gift to humanity," he told the children. "Yes, he confiscated our passports to eternity. His theory offers no solace to those who say we're embryonic angels, headed for heaven. Ah, but he gave us something more valuable in return. He gave us citizenship papers. 'We aren't tourists on this planet,' Darwin's theory tells us. 'The earth is our home. We belong here.'"

Sonya had no idea how her effort to liberate the abridged reincarnation of Mr. Darwin would play out. Quite possibly the Rowens would hunt him down and drag him back to the carnival. But even if the worst happened, she knew Uncle Kostos would be proud of her and Vasily for attempting to deliver this paragon of scientists from the red-button man.

After Mr. Darwin availed himself of the men's room, the rescue party squeezed into a booth at Viva Zapata, a tight fit for the gorilla. The manager, who reminded Sonya of Wallace Beery playing Long John Silver, sauntered over, glowered, and muttered something about public health ordinances, but then a waitress reminiscent of the glamorous Lupe Vélez appeared, and Celeste cleverly ordered, on Mr. Darwin's behalf, what probably amounted to a barrel of frijoles wrapped in twenty pounds of tortillas. Thus was the manager appeased.

The food arrived promptly, and everyone dug in. When her brother requested his second alcoholic concoction, tequila with orange juice, Sonya was hardly surprised, as he'd gone all day without a drop. Everyone else, including Mr. Darwin, opted for bottles of Corona and Dos Equis.

When not gobbling down vegetarian tacos, Mr. Darwin scribbled messages.

CORONA EXCELLENT BEVERAGE.

Listing affectionately toward Sonya, Homer pointed to the ape. "Wait till he finds out about tequila."

BAMBOO SHOOTS FOR DESSERT?

"I'm afraid that's not on the menu," said Sonya.

CIGARETTE?

Vasily pulled out a pack of Chesterfields along with a box of safety matches. He shook the pack, deftly causing a single cigarette to emerge. Clumsily the gorilla snatched it up.

I HATE BEING HALF OF ME, wrote Mr. Darwin as Vasily lit the cigarette.

"That's understandable," said Homer.

The gorilla took a drag. WHERE IS REST OF ME?

"Probably with the Rowens," said Vasily.

MAKE ME WHOLE.

"I don't even know where they live," said Vasily.

"The Ennis House in Los Feliz," said Celeste. "I was there in March, rehearsing my Sister Torrance routine."

GET REST OF ME TONIGHT OR I GO TO KITCHEN AND URINATE IN CHILI POT.

"I think we owe him the other half of his brain," said Homer.

I DEFECATE ON TORTILLAS.

"A trip to Los Feliz wouldn't be out the question," said Sonya. "We hornswoggled Pollock. We can do the same to the Rowens."

HELP ME, DR. ORLOV.

Without warning a sharp bang reverberated through the restaurant. A pistol report, Sonya realized as the scent of saltpeter coiled into her nostrils. She lurched out of the booth along with Vasily, Homer, and Celeste.

A short, stocky man wearing a black mask and a Panama hat stood before the cash register, training a smoking revolver on Lupe Vélez's terrified lookalike, hands raised high as if she were trying to stop traffic. Plaster sifted down from the ceiling into which the desperado had evidently fired a warning shot. Wallace Beery's double hovered protectively beside the waitress.

"If anybody interferes," the desperado shouted, "this lovely señorita gets a bullet in the head!" He handed a paper sack to Wallace Beery. "Gimme all the folding money you got."

As Mr. Darwin exited the booth, the manager opened the cash register drawer and began filling the sack with bills. The gorilla rose to full height and growled.

"Hurry up!" demanded the desperado.

The angry ape bounded across the restaurant, his extended arms pantomiming strangulation. The desperado dropped his revolver. Mr. Darwin bared his large, white, vegetarian teeth. The customers shrieked. With balled fists the gorilla pounded on his great tympani of a chest, then opened his mouth and roared, the echoes filling the restaurant like a thunderclap.

Ignoring the sack of money, the desperado pivoted on his heel and sprinted out the door, whereupon the customers cheered and whooped.

Homer strode toward the counter, picked up the

revolver, and swung open the cylinder. "You can all pay us back by patronizing *Tarzan and the City of Gold*"—he shook the five remaining bullets into his palm—"starring Johnny Weissmuller and Zolgar here, coming soon to a theater near you!" He jammed the gun and the ammo into his pocket.

"Needless to say, your dinners are on the house," said Wallace Beery to the gorilla and his human companions. "And you can have all the tequila you can drink."

The customers applauded.

"Even I can't drink all the tequila I can drink," said Vasily.

"Thank you, Señor," said Homer, "but our director expects us to wake up bright-eyed and bushy-tailed for the elephant stampede."

"And now we must bid you *adios*," said Sonya, "for we have a shooting schedule to keep and miles to go before we sleep."

But not too many miles, as it happened, for it took them less than an hour to reach their destination in Los Feliz. Illuminated by a golden moon, the Ennis House, an architectural marvel keyed to the Mayan Revival style, emerged in concrete splendor from the side of a wooded hill. The sign on the roof read *Jubilee Publishing Company*.

Celeste explained that the house had been designed by Frank Lloyd Wright in 1924 for a successful husband-and-wife team of haberdashers. Exasperated with the maintenance costs, Charles and Mabel Ennis eventually moved out and started renting the place to Hollywood producers as a movie set and to socialites for lavish parties, but now they leased it exclusively to the Rowens.

Sonya parked in the Ennis House motor court. Antique gas lamps spangled the terrazzo walkway to the portico. Vasily rang the bell on the colossal front door, which swung open to reveal an elegant black man dressed in a butler's charcoal morning coat.

"Are you expected?" he asked in a melodious voice.

"No," said Sonya.

"That's rather the point," said Vasily.

"Hello, Jordan," said Celeste. "Remember me? It's imperative we chat with Nigel and Desmond."

"Nice to see you again, Sister Torrance," said the butler. "Brother Zolgar, I hope you've been well."

Mr. Darwin roared and thumped his chest.

Jordan guided the visitors through a labyrinth of corridors filled with sealed cardboard cartons stacked like sandbags in a Great War trench, each labeled *Exploring Creation through Biology* followed by *Quantity: 24* and *Jubilee Publishing*. An unseen organist filled the halls with some sort of church music, the somber chords increasing in volume as the group entered a darkened parlor that served as a movie theater. The screen displayed a black-and-white Nativity scene. Dust motes drifted in the spray of light coming from the projection booth. Sofas, divans, and loveseats were scattered about the room, interspersed with still more book cartons.

Jordan opened the booth door and switched off the

projector. The Nativity vanished. The organ died. The butler worked a rheostat, and the glow of a chandelier filled the parlor. Nigel and Desmond Rowen, both in late middle-age and wearing identical green velvet smoking jackets, rose from leather armchairs and scowled at their guests. With their strong chins, aquiline noses, and dark hair streaked with white, Sonya thought them quite handsome in a discomfiting Bela Lugosi sort of way.

"Hi, there, Nigel, sorry to interrupt," said Celeste to the elder Rowen.

"Young lady, what brings you and Brother Zolgar here at this time of night?" he asked, affecting an aristocratic accent. "You've got five shows in Pomona tomorrow."

"The monkey and I are quitting the circus," said Celeste with a pixie smile. "Find yourselves another Evangelical Wonder."

Mr. Darwin growled.

"Replacing your Primate Prophet will be easy," said Vasily. "Or have you sworn off kidnapping apes and upgrading their brains?"

The Rowens stiffened in unison. "I would offer you some refreshment, Dr. Orlov," said Nigel, "but we're all out of bathtub vodka."

"Liquor is legal again," noted Vasily.

"We'll remember that for your next visit."

"Sister Torrance, you picked an inconvenient hour to renegotiate your contract," said Desmond. "We've just started screening *Ben-Hur*—the 1931 re-release with the synched organ track."

"I'm not here to renegotiate my contract," said Celeste.

"Our man at Metro struck a 16mm print just for us," said Nigel. "*Ben-Hur* was Hollywood's finest hour. I actually had a bit part."

"As a horse's ass?" said Vasily.

"As our Savior," said Nigel tartly. "My face was never shown."

"*My* face is shown all the time," said Sonya. "Ever seen a Nocturnia picture? A Golemoiselle?"

"Ah, so you're that monster movie actress your brother told us so much about," said Nigel. "Can't you find more wholesome things to do with your time?"

"And this is my boyfriend, Homer, who writes *Ticket to Tomorrow*. Not your sort of fare, either."

"Zolgar will now explain our presence here," said Vasily.

Mr. Darwin approached the Rowens, encircled their waists with his mighty arms, and bent forward, so that they now hung upside down as if their legs were hooked around adjacent trapezes.

"Let me go!" cried Nigel, kicking.

Jordan started toward his inverted employers, halting abruptly when Homer pulled out the revolver he'd retrieved from the failed holdup. Even though the bullet chambers were now empty, he made a point of aiming it at the ceiling.

"Tell us where to find the rest of Mr. Darwin's brain," said Vasily.

"I can't give directions upside down!" protested Nigel.

"Make an effort," said Sonya.

"Basement!" gasped Desmond. "Refrigerator! Ice chest!"

"Zolgar will now set you upright," said Vasily. "Jordan will then lead Celeste and Homer to the basement."

Mr. Darwin released the brothers. As they found their footing and regained their dignity, Jordan guided Celeste and Homer out of the room.

"News flash," said Sonya. "This afternoon I bought your act from Sam Pollock."

"You *bought* it?" whined Nigel.

"He had no right to sell it," moaned Desmond.

"I gave him a big, fat, personal check," said Sonya. "Public adulation pays well these days."

"Now tell us why you wanted Charles Darwin's brain in an ape," said Vasily.

"None of your business," said Desmond.

"I'll bet Zolgar could jiggle an answer out of you," said Sonya.

The gorilla bellowed and pounded on a book carton.

"Shall I go first?" said Nigel, wincing, and Desmond nodded. "No sooner had Darwin published his book than evolutionists declared war on the Church of England."

"Actually I think it was the other way around," said Sonya.

"Everybody remembers how Darwin's favorite sycophant, Thomas Henry Huxley, embarrassed Bishop Wilberforce during the big showdown at Oxford," said Nigel. "But later that year our grandfather, the great anatomist and paleontologist Sir Robert Rowen—"

"Who gave the world the word 'dinosaur,'" noted Desmond.

"Grandfather *also* suffered an injustice at Huxley's hands. For years Sir Robert had argued that the great apes are discontinuous with humans, for our brains alone possess a *hippocampus minor* and a *posterior cornu*. So Huxley, the knave, arranged a series of public dissections at which many an alleged gorilla *hippocampus* and *cornu* were laid bare."

"What you call an injustice I would call getting the facts right," said Vasily.

Nigel proceeded to tell how Sir Robert, acting on his conviction that brain transplants would one day become a reality, had in April of 1882 visited Charles Darwin's sickroom in Kent, where the scientist lay dying of heart failure. Sir Robert had informed the vigil keepers—Mrs. Darwin and three of the couple's grown children—that he and Mr. Darwin had overcome their professional animosity, and now he wanted to try saving his brilliant colleague. Her husband's "neurocardiac fever," he believed, might be cured through an emergency trepanning. Emma Darwin gave her consent.

After clearing the room, Robert Rowen and two assistants had anesthetized the patient, removed his entire brain, and secured it in an ice locker. When Emma returned, Sir Robert tearfully explained that Charles had passed away before the procedure could be completed. With Emma's blessing, Sir Robert applied theatrical makeup to the corpse's brow, thus sparing future mourners the sight of the incision. To wit, it was an empty skull that the pallbearers had carried, along with the rest of Darwin's remains, to Westminster Abbey for interment.

"Sir Robert outlived his wife and, sadly, his own son, our father," said Desmond. "Our mother was the only person by his side when he died. He told her to entrust his two grandsons with a momentous commission. Once medical science had progressed far enough, we must arrange for Darwin's left hemisphere to wind up in an orangutan or a gorilla."

"Thus would Grandfather's nemesis find himself in a hell wrought by his own vile theory of primate neurological equivalence," said Nigel. "Half human, half ape, perpetually incomplete, unimaginably frustrated, eternally humiliated."

As the gorilla howled pitifully, the search party returned. Homer and Jordan carried between them a steel chest festooned with rivets. Celeste gripped a bottle of Corona, presumably from the basement refrigerator.

The instant he saw the brain receptacle, Mr. Darwin cavorted joyfully around the room.

"In time we'll forgive you for robbing us at gunpoint," said Nigel.

"Confiscating a stolen brain hardly qualifies as robbery," noted Sonya.

"We'll have more trouble forgiving you for interfering with our grandfather's dying request."

Sonya rapped her knuckles on the nearest carton. "But Sir Robert would be pleased with these."

"He didn't commission us to write textbooks,"

Desmond replied curtly. "What he cared about was the location of his worst enemy's left cortical hemisphere."

"Nevertheless, it looks like Jubilee Publishing is doing all right."

"Last month we got adopted by the Texas Board of Education," said Nigel, smirking. "Thanks to the Scopes verdict, nearly every biology textbook being published in America these days is silent on the subject of evolution—and ours is the quietest of all."

The gorilla started howling again.

"WHAT WOULD THEIR VERDICT BE?"
—*The Daily Star* (Montreal).

With his penknife Desmond slit open a carton and removed a copy of *Exploring Creation through Biology*. "Today Texas, tomorrow the whole USA!" He placed the volume in Vasily's grasp. "Keep it. You might learn something."

Mr. Darwin reached into the carton, grabbed a book, and pressed it to his chest like a poultice.

"I urge you to read it," Desmond instructed the ape. "You'll realize how wrong you were."

Mr. Darwin snarled.

Owing to the dense fog and relentless rain, it took Sonya a full hour to transport her companions to Medusa Manor, an imitation *castillo* of stucco and limestone. She secured the ice chest in the Frigidaire. Keyed up by the day's escapades, the group spontaneously huddled in the conservatory, where the housekeeper, Mrs. Blackwood, served them coffee and cognac—and still more coffee and cognac—while discreetly saying nothing about the gorilla in the room.

"I suggest we do the procedure promptly, before the Rowens go to the police and insist we stole a precious heirloom," said Vasily. "We can't have some flatfoot barging in during the operation."

"Though we could try seizing the high ground," said Sonya. " 'Yes, officer, we're indeed transplanting half a human brain into a gorilla, but it belonged to a long-dead scientist, not the Rowens, so maybe you should go find a missing child or something.' "

WANT HUMAN VOCAL CORDS, wrote Mr. Darwin on a page from Pollock's screenplay.

"That will be difficult," said Vasily.

I MUST SPEAK.

"While you're under the ether, I'll attempt to modify your larynx."

GOING INSANE.

"I'll try my damndest."

THAT MEANS YOU STAY SOBER.

Although Medusa Manor had several guest suites, everyone was too inebriated and exhausted to climb the stairs, so Mrs. Blackwood simply dumped pillows, quilts, and blankets on the floor. Thus did the mansion become the scene of a slumber party, though it took Sonya over an hour to fall asleep, so vivid were the images of cheerful Siamese twins and literate lowland gorillas cascading through her skull.

The five of them slept till noon. While Mrs. Blackwood served everyone frankfurters for lunch, Vasily got on the phone to Nurse Cassidy, telling her to prepare for a brain transplant and collateral laryngeal surgery.

By the time the group reached the Orlov Clinic, the afternoon sky had darkened and heavy weather was brewing. Vasily pulled on rubber gloves and transferred Mr. Darwin's right cerebral hemisphere from the ice chest to a large glass beaker. Leaving the cortical matter to thaw in his steam-heated greenhouse, he guided everyone up the tower stairs to the dome-covered turret he'd converted into a surgical theater. Evidently determined to write messages until the moment of anesthetization, Mr. Darwin brought along Pollock's screenplay.

With its dented steel operating table, spavined instrument cabinet, and ancient bricks peeking through leprous plaster, the place seemed to Sonya more like a Golemoiselle set than a venue for real-world brain transplants. She half expected a deranged alchemist to appear and start reciting incantations. At least the lighting was adequate, an array of kliegs and pinspots Vasily had probably bought at a B-studio fire sale.

Dressed in a crisp, bleached nurse's uniform, Yvonne Cassidy, a pretty, moonfaced woman with bee-stung lips, was laying out the essential paraphernalia atop a credenza: electric razor, ether cone, bone saw, vascular clamps, hemostats, retractors, sponges, dressings.

"Hello again, Mr. Zolgar," she said.

HELLO TO YOU, wrote the gorilla.

Yvonne grabbed a checklist affixed to a clipboard and, exuding an aura of expertise leavened with tenderness, started ticking off items.

SCARED.

"A normal human response," Yvonne assured the gorilla.

Slipping on his surgical gown, Vasily announced that henceforth Celeste would be addressed as Nurse Torrance. He outlined the procedure step by step, noting that the laryngeal alterations would probably prove even more challenging than the hemisphere swap, then assigned everyone a duty. While Nurse Cassidy administered the anesthesia drop by drop and passed instruments to Vasily,

Nurse Torrance would sponge up the patient's blood and the surgeon's sweat. Homer's job would be to redirect the pinspots as needed. Sonya was charged with looking out the window and making sure nobody was bringing an emergency case to the clinic.

Nurse Cassidy now performed the most essential preoperative task, taking up the electric razor and shaving hanks of hair from Mr. Darwin's throat, brow, and cranium, so that his head now suggested a wooded mountain with a bare summit rising above the timberline.

The patient and the surgical team descended to the dining room and, exchanging no words, sat down at a mahogany table. Nurse Cassidy served them cold chicken and German potato salad, admonishing Mr. Darwin not to consume even one morsel.

APE BRAIN IS ON MY RIGHT, he wrote. THAT'S THE HALF YOU'RE REMOVING.

"Thanks for the reminder," said Vasily.

HOW WILL I FEEL?

"Like last time, you'll have a headache," said Vasily. "Your throat will hurt. We'll give you aspirin. And you'll have to remain silent for a week."

Yvonne directed Sonya, Homer, and Celeste into the lavatory and required them to scour their hands and forearms to the point of chafing. After the team put on surgical gloves, everyone mounted the tower staircase, Nurse Cassidy carrying the partially thawed hemisphere in its beaker, Nurse Torrance bearing a soup tureen intended for the right half of Zolgar's cerebrum.

Shortly after they stepped into the theater, an

uncommon meteorological event for Southern California, an electrical storm, broke over Los Angeles. Thunderclaps shook the turret, rattling the window panes and jangling the surgical instruments. Yvonne took the tureen from Sonya, placed it on the floor, and distributed white surgical face masks. Mr. Darwin climbed gingerly onto the table, whereupon Vasily stippled his brow with red ink.

As Nurse Torrance strapped the ether cone over the gorilla's nose, Nurse Cassidy opened the anesthesia bottle. A blistering fragrance invaded the room, like the smell of a thousand bananas gone bad. Sonya had never before inhaled so aggressive an odor. If ether were a sound, it would have been a scream.

She breathed deeply, hoping to clear the chemical from her brain, and stationed herself by the casement. Windshield wipers sluicing furiously, a steady line of cars crawled down Loch Lomond Drive, but there were no visitors in sight.

The thunder became a cannonade. The lighting set the theater aglow. Vasily, undaunted, worked slowly and steadily. After the first hour, Homer threw up, then went back to directing the pinspots as if nothing had happened.

Sonya was glad to be posted so far away, knowing that, like Homer, she would have found the sight nauseating. She was tempted to stuff cotton in her ears but decided she was obligated to keep all her senses engaged—and so she endured the staccato clicks of steel on bone as the knife connected the ink dots, the suck of the scalp being peeled from the skull, the shriek of the bone saw, the sloshy protest of the fascia as the cranium came free, the plop of the simian hemisphere entering the tureen, and the squeal of the needle suturing up the patient's scalp and throat.

"Okay, it's finished," said Vasily. "Brain upgraded, larynx successfully modified—at least I think so."

Nurse Torrance mopped his brow.

"Well done, Dr. Orlov," gushed Nurse Cassidy.

"I even cut out the damn electrode," noted Vasily.

"Sorry I threw up," muttered Homer.

"You did?" said Nurse Torrance.

"I need a drink," said Vasily.

On Sunday afternoon Celeste moved into the guest cottage at Medusa Manor. "In my home town, your bungalow would pass for a rich person's house," she remarked to Sonya.

Now an official member of the Orlov Clinic staff, Celeste got up at the crack of dawn on Monday and took the bus to Pico Rivera. Returning that evening, she reported that the patient was doing splendidly, though he remained under strict orders not to speak.

Because Tuesday's shooting schedule involved only non-Golemoiselle scenes, Mr. Ferris allowed Sonya to take the morning off so she could visit Mr. Darwin. Proud of his role in the astounding procedure, Homer came along. Dressed in a billowing white hospital johnny, looking by turns alert, groggy, and poleaxed, the patient was still confined to the recovery room. Bandages enswathed his brow and neck, giving him the appearance of a sixteenth-century philosopher in a scholar's cap and matching Elizabethan collar.

"Until his throat has mended," said Celeste, reveling in her new identity as an angel of mercy, "he mustn't say even one word. Right, Mr. Darwin?"

The gorilla man nodded.

"Swelling, infection, and rejection are under control," said Yvonne.

"He's allowed only vegetable broth and sips of brandy," noted Celeste.

Vasily entered the recovery room bearing a box of chalk and a slate the size of a checkerboard.

"Mr. Darwin, do you understand what's happened to you?"

The gorilla man sat up in bed, then lifted a hairy hand and moved his fingers as if playing a harp. He grabbed a piece of chalk and began writing. His letters were straighter than Brother Zolgar's but fell short of adult human penmanship.

I HAVE BEEN MADE WHOLE.

"Your powers of intuition, creativity, and music appreciation will presumably become as strong as in your previous life," said Vasily. "And I altered your larynx as best I could."

RIGHT BRAIN MUSICAL?

"That's what the literature on brain injuries suggests."

LEFT BRAIN LINGUISTIC?

"Apparently."

Mr. Darwin erased the slate with a stray piece of gauze.

WE HAD A PIANO. EMMA PLAYED FOR ME.

Saltwater trickled down both hairy cheeks. Vasily had evidently installed the hemisphere without damaging the connection between Mr. Darwin's mind and his tear ducts.

WRITING DIFFICULT. WISH FINGERS WEREN'T TO THICK.

"Maybe we could give him a hand transplant, like what happened to Colin Clive in *Mad Love*," said Homer.

Again the gorilla man erased the slate.

NO MORE SURGERY.

"I quite agree," said Vasily.

A spasm of satisfaction rushed through Sonya. Her decision to have Mr. Darwin come live at Medusa Manor, she mused, was farsighted and astute. She anticipated the ambience, at once primeval and intellectual, he would bring to the place, and if Homer didn't like the arrangement, *tant pis*.

"My largest guest suite awaits you," she said.

Mr. Darwin worked his simian lips into a smile.

EYES FUNCTION BETTER THAN WHEN I WAS ZOLGAR. I INTEND TO READ ROWEN TEXT.

"I'd recommend against it," said Vasily.

"That book will only cause you distress," said Sonya.

"Forget the Rowens," said Homer.

I MUST READ IT.

Exactly one week after the procedure, Vasily decided to let Mr. Darwin use his modified vocal cords. He was now spending several hours a day in a rocking chair, though he took frequent naps and continued to wear his hospital johnny.

After his well-wishers had gathered around the rocker, Vasily brushed Mr. Darwin's bandaged neck with his fingertips.

"Now speak."

The gorilla man cupped his throat and clucked his tongue.

"Ch-ch-ch…," he rasped.

"Good," said Vasily. "A phoneme."

"Ch-ch-ch…"

"Chocolate?" suggested Sonya.

"Cherries?" Celeste guessed.

"Ch-ch-ch-children."

"What about them?" said Vasily.

"I had t-t-ten … ch-children."

"He can talk!" shouted Celeste.

"Bravo!" cried Homer.

"And I'm sure they were all very proud of you," said Sonya.

Mr. Darwin opened his eyes. "Mary d-died after b-birth. Charlie n-never saw third b-birthday. Annie never saw eleventh. Consumption. I w-wonder what h-happened to the others."

"I'll try to find out," said Homer.

"Henrietta, Elizabeth, Leonard, William, Francis, Horace, and George."

"Golly," said Celeste.

"Victorian gentlemen favored large families," Homer explained.

"You c-call us Victorians?" Mr. Darwin rubbed the bandages encircling his throat. "My v-voice sounds strange."

"You'll get used to it," said Vasily.

"My Uncle Kostos idolizes you," said Sonya. "He taught my siblings and me about the Darwinian tree of life."

"The D-Darwinian tree? He uses that t-term?"

"He says you confiscated our passports to heaven, but you gave us citizenship papers in return. We're not tourists. The earth is our home."

"Most g-gratifying. I assume your uncle is not from T-Tennessee."

"Smolensk."

"*State of T-Tennessee versus Scopes...*" Mr. Darwin began rocking back and forth. "Was Scopes found g-guilty, like the Rowens taught me to say?"

"Guilty, yes," said Homer.

"He in fact violated the Butler Act," said Celeste. "'It shall be unlawful to teach any theory that denies the story of the Divine Creation of Man as taught in the Bible...'"

"Was Scopes h-hanged?"

"He was fined a hundred dollars," said Celeste.

"I thought p-perhaps they hanged scofflaws in Tennessee."

"Only the descendants of slaves," said Homer.

"That's horrible," said Mr. Darwin. "I remember when Mr. Lincoln issued his Emancipation Proclamation. Front p-page of the *Times*. We were b-born on the same day in 1809."

"The verdict of history is that you were both great men," said Homer.

"Though that is not the v-verdict in Tennessee," observed Mr. Darwin.

"I wonder who's hated more in Nashville, Memphis, and Knoxville today," said Homer. "Charles Darwin or Abraham Lincoln?"

"The Tennessee Supreme Court upheld the constitutionality of the Butler Act," said Celeste, "but overturned Scopes's conviction on a technicality."

"Is it still the law of that land?" asked Mr. Darwin.

Celeste shrugged.

"I'll do the research," said Homer.

"This is all so strange," said Mr. Darwin. "I feel as if I've been on a sabbatical from myself."

"And now at last it's over," said Vasily. "Welcome back to *Homo sapiens*."

"Dr. Orlov, I am eternally in your debt. I hope to use my second life wisely."

CHAPTER 3
DR. PONGOWANA'S FORGOTTEN ANCESTORS

Ten days after Charles Darwin became, as far as anyone knew, the world's only talking gorilla, Sonya received a telegram from her brother saying the patient was ready to be discharged. All during the drive to the Orlov Clinic, she kept telling Homer how gratifying it felt to be helping her Uncle Kostos's scientific hero. He reacted with icy silence. Was the dear boy jealous? Did he fear she would find the exotic Mr. Darwin more fascinating than a mere radio drama writer? She decided she must reassure him of her devotion, though not quite yet.

They entered the sundrenched convalescent room to find Celeste dressed in a starched white uniform and fully inhabiting her Nurse Torrance persona. Brow fixed in a professional frown, she unwound the bandages from Mr. Darwin's head and throat. The gorilla man's moist eyes sparkled with good cheer, and his fur exuded an earthy, beguiling scent.

"Now that we're all friends," he said, "you should call me 'Charles.'"

Celeste slid a mercury thermometer into his mouth, cautioning him not to bite down.

"I suspect I'll always think of you as 'Mr. Darwin,'" said Sonya.

MR. BERGH TO THE RESCUE.

THE DEFRAUDED GORILLA. "That *Man* wants to claim my Pedigree. He says he is one of my Descendants."
Mr. BERGH. "Now, Mr. DARWIN, how could you insult him so?"

"And I'll probably keep calling you 'sir,'" said Homer,

"'Charles was my late father's name," said Celeste. "The Reverend Charles Emmanuel Torrance, God's ambassador to Southern California." She removed the thermometer and scrutinized the calibrations. "Ninety degrees Fahrenheit, perfectly normal for your ... species."

"Make sure he gets lots of rest and sticks to a liquid diet until his larynx heals," Vasily told Sonya.

"What about cigarettes?" asked Mr. Darwin.

"Verboten," said Vasily.

Later, as they climbed into the back seat of the Studebaker, Homer offered Mr. Darwin a Chesterfield. He declined it with a wave of his hand.

"I'm determined to obey my doctor's orders. He's obviously more competent than the quacks I knew in the previous century."

"What about his order not to read the Rowens' textbook?" asked Sonya as they started down Loch Lomond Drive.

"I'm wondering what Mr. Chilton learned about the Butler Act," said Mr. Darwin, ignoring her question.

"It's still in force," said Homer, "likewise a Mississippi statute forbidding science teachers to discuss evolution, and Arkansas recently passed a referendum banning so-called monkey curricula."

Mr. Darwin's growl reverberated through the Studebaker.

"Tell him about his descendants," said Sonya.

"Leonard is still with us at age eighty-five," said Homer. "After serving in the Intelligence Division of the Ministry of War, he stood for Parliament and won. Eventually he left office to head the Royal Geological Society."

"I'm tempted to cross the ocean and seek out the old

fellow," said Mr. Darwin, "but I fear the shock might kill him."

"Your firstborn son, William, remained a banker in Southampton until his retirement. Your second-born, George, is remembered as one of England's greatest geophysicists. Francis became a botany professor. Horace founded the Cambridge Scientific Instrument Company."

"Four scientists and a banker. Impressive. Let me guess. Elizabeth never amounted to anything, but Henrietta left her mark."

"She edited your wife's letters for publication. All your grandchildren, I'm delighted to say, are still alive, including the five you know about and the four you never got to meet."

"None of whom would be pleased to encounter a gorilla who claimed to be their grandfather."

"I would have to agree, sir," said Homer.

"And Emma? I would hope that she…"

"Your wife enjoyed a long and comfortable life, passing away at the ripe old age of eighty-eight," said Homer.

"Sleep well, my darling," said Mr. Darwin.

Upon their arrival at the estate, Sonya led the gorilla man up the grand staircase to his suite. Because she was supposed to be on the set of *Moon of the She-Wolf*, she instructed Mrs. Blackwood to teach their guest about the bathtub faucets, give him his linens, and show him his closets. Thanks to Sonya's industry and the efforts of a half-dozen seamstresses, Mr. Darwin could choose from a collection of day-shirts, caftans, and dressing gowns,

Celeste having discreetly taken his measurements right after the procedure.

When Sonya got home that night, Homer at her side, she found an agitated gorilla man shambling around the library wearing her favorite piece from his new collection, a silk robe embroidered with stylized Chinese dragons.

"What twaddle!" he wailed, brandishing his copy of *Exploring Creation through Biology*, which he'd evidently perused in defiance of Vasily's directive. He cracked the spine and read, " 'Darwin's conjectures amount to a restatement of Jean-Baptist de Lamarck's discredited theory of the inheritance of acquired characteristics.' Such tommyrot!"

"Complete piffle," said Sonya.

"Very well, in *The Origin of Species* I *did* posit that Lamarckian principles of use and disuse might be subsidiary forces in evolution, but the mechanism of descent is natural selection. My book is a *riposte* to Lamarck and his inane metaphysics!"

"I heard shouting," said Celeste, entering the room.

"'Darwin correctly maintained that primitive forms came into existence before complex ones,' " the gorilla man read, " 'with one-celled green plants preceding one-celled animals, worms antedating anacondas, and so on, for we learn in Genesis that God made His creatures in an orderly fashion. The grasses, plants, and trees that appeared on Day Three were supplemented on Day Five by birds, fish, and great whales, and then came Man on Day Six.' Poppycock!"

"I don't disagree," said Homer.

"If I understood what the Rowens told us," said Mr. Darwin, "American biology texts pretend my theory doesn't even exist."

"In my Life Sciences class at Hollywood High," said Celeste, nodding, "we studied taxonomy and dissected a frog."

"Our biology teacher gave a ten-minute lecture on evolution right before summer vacation," said Homer. "Nobody heard a word."

"The youth of America have a right to know about the fundamental unity of all living things!" the gorilla man declared.

The youth of America. The phrase brought an unexpected lump to Sonya's throat. Until that moment, she hadn't quite realized how patriotic she'd become, how fiercely the Statue of Liberty's lamp burned in her breast. God bless all those earnest and callow American moviegoers who'd made her Hollywood's horror queen.

"Mr. Darwin, it occurs to me that this nation's youth might be learning about your tree of life *outside* the classroom," she said. "There's a line about 'the Darwinian theory' in a recent horror movie called *The Monster Walks*."

"What's a movie?"

"Short for 'moving picture,'" said Homer. "Rather like a magic-lantern show, only more kinetic. Miss Orlova earns her living acting in them. Think of that Nativity scene the Rowens were watching in their parlor."

"And *The Monster Walks* is a whore movie?" said Mr. Darwin. "Sounds salacious."

"*Horror* movie—a melodrama about people coping with darkly romantic supernatural forces," said Sonya.

"Do most horror movies treat of evolution?"

"Some do, yes," said Homer. "*The Island of Lost Souls* gave us Dr. Moreau, a scientist who tries to turn animals into people. *Murders in the Rue Morgue* opens with Dr. Mirakle lecturing about the missing link."

"I've always detested that term, 'missing link,'" said Mr. Darwin. "The tree of life is not a *chain*."

"Perhaps if you actually *saw* these movies, you'd feel better," said Sonya.

"Perhaps," said Mr. Darwin.

"Isaac Bachman knows I'm the main reason Excelsior has so far survived this depression," said Sonya. "If I tell him to arrange private screenings of *Lost Souls* and *Rue Morgue*, he'll make it happen."

"Before the festival, I'll give him a list of some other inadvertently educational potboilers," said Homer.

"Bring on the horror movies," said Mr. Darwin. "Give me Dr. Moreau and Dr. Mirakle. I feel a professional kinship with them already."

On a dark and stormy Friday night in August of 1935, Sonya ushered Homer, Celeste, and Mr. Darwin into the Excelsior projection room. The festival began with *The Island of Lost Souls*, 1932, based on *The Island of Dr. Moreau*, H.G. Wells's novel about a vivisectionist seeking to accelerate mammalian evolution by imposing on his subjects successive approximations of the human form. Having learned that Wells had been a student of Thomas Henry Huxley, the scientist who'd clashed with the Rowens' grandfather over the neurological continuity between gorillas and humans, Sonya figured the film might very well do justice to Mr. Darwin's theory.

The big expository scene found Charles Laughton as Dr. Moreau lecturing Richard Arlen playing a castaway named Edward Parker. "I started with plant life twenty years ago. I took an orchid and stripped a hundred thousand years of slow evolution from it, until I no longer had an orchid but what orchids will become many millennia from now."

"A scientist who thinks he changed an orchid into a foreordained future version of itself understands nothing about evolution," Mr. Darwin protested. "Orchids aren't *destined* to become anything. That's the whole *point*."

"This isn't a completely faithful adaptation of Mr. Wells's book," noted Homer.

"I let my imagination run fantastically ahead," said Moreau. "Why not experiment with more complex organisms? Man is the present climax of a long process of organic evolution. All animal life is tending toward the human form."

"Human beings aren't the climax of evolution," objected Mr. Darwin. "Animal life is no more tending toward *Homo sapiens* than it's tending toward buttered scones. I hope this tinpot Jehovah's hybrids turn against him."

As it happened, he got his wish. The picture ended

with Moreau's menagerie cornering him in his House of Pain and practicing on his own person what they'd taught him about vivisection.

On Saturday morning Homer threaded up the Edgar Allan Poe adaptation, *Murders in the Rue Morgue*, also 1932. In the first scene, two nineteenth-century medical students, the dreamy Pierre and the worldly Paul, attended a nocturnal carnival in Paris. After surveying the mountebanks and bunko artists, the students escorted their lady friends through the arched loins of a huge painted gorilla toward an attraction billed as Erik the Ape Man.

Inside the theater, bushy-browed Dr. Mirakle, played by Bela Lugosi, stood before a mural illustrating the thirteen stages through which one-celled animals had supposedly traveled as they gradually transmuted into human beings. "I'm not exhibiting a freak, a monstrosity of Nature, but a milestone in the development of life," Mirakle insisted. "The shadow of Erik the Ape hangs over us all, the darkness before the dawn of Man."

A brutish assistant pulled the curtain away from Erik's cage, and a snarling simian face filled the screen. The filmmakers, to Sonya's annoyance, had settled for a blurry close-up of a chimpanzee, though a satisfying long-shot followed showing an actor in an orangutan suit.

"Here is the story of Man," said Dr. Mirakle, indicating his mural. "In the slime of chaos, there was a seed that grew into the tree of life. Fins changed into wings, wings into ears. Crawling reptiles grew legs. Eons of ages passed. There came a time when a four-legged thing walked erect. Behold the first man!"

"That isn't right," grumbled Mr. Darwin. "That isn't even wrong."

"But isn't it satisfying to hear the great Bela Lugosi expound upon your tree of life?" asked Sonya.

"Mirakle should talk about the *mechanism* behind evolution. Unsolicited but advantageous variations confer reproductive fitness on particular individuals, with consequent propagation of desirable traits."

"He probably said that in the rough cut," remarked Homer.

Back in their garret, Paul admonished Pierre for living inside his head. "Your eyes are getting glassy! Just like that old charlatan's!"

"Did you pay attention to what he said?" asked Paul.

"You mean about us being the product of evolution?"

"Has it occurred to you he might be right?"

"Eat your lunch!"

"No, Pierre, don't eat your lunch!" fumed Mr. Darwin. "Better to starve than promulgate a garbled account of human descent. I hope the ape strangles his owner."

Once again, Mr. Darwin got his wish.

That afternoon they screened *The Monster Walks*, likewise 1932, which found the villain plotting to cheat his niece out of her inheritance by murdering her and diverting suspicion to his late mad-scientist brother's experimental subject, a chimpanzee caged in the cellar. In the final beats, a black chauffeur pointed to the imprisoned ape and asked the family lawyer why anyone "would keep one of them things around the house."

"Dr. Earlton was an exponent of the Darwinian theory," the lawyer replied. "He believed they were our ancestors."

"You mean he's related to me?" asked the chauffeur.

"Exactly."

"Well, I don't know. I had a grandpappy that looked something like him, but he wasn't as active."

"Enough!" cried Mr. Darwin. "Shut it off!"

But the film had already ended.

"*The Monster Walks* is a gross insult to the Negro race!" bellowed Mr. Darwin. "As for the notion that chimpanzees are ancestral to humans, to call that evolutionary theory is like calling a woodcutter's hut the Taj Mahal."

"Next comes *The Beast of Borneo*," said Homer. "A deranged physician captures a live orangutan to prove that humans emerged from earlier primates."

"This festival is over!" seethed Mr. Darwin. "Finis!"

"We could screen *The Lost World* instead. It has an ape man, plus dinosaurs fighting each other through the magic of stop-motion animation."

"No more travesties!"

"If a horror film is ever going to present your theory accurately, sir, we'll just have to make it ourselves," said Sonya idly.

"Ourselves?" said Mr. Darwin. "Can we do that?"

The notion suddenly struck her fancy. "I don't see why not …"

"What a delicious idea," said Celeste.

"Though woefully impractical," said Homer.

"Impractical, yes—but then so was my ambition to become a movie star," said Sonya. "Mr. Darwin, with your permission, I'd like to try writing a screenplay that does right by your ideas."

"Of course you have my permission."

"And also your collaboration, perhaps? Work with me, sir, and soon we'll have a script worth showing to Isaac Bachman."

"Sonya, forgive me," said Homer, "but this all sounds quite nutty."

"I prefer the term 'patriotic.' I want to repay America's youth for blessing me with so rewarding a career."

"Except they don't *want* to be repaid, darling—not *that* way," said Homer. "Give the kids lots of thrills and as much sex as you can get away with. Science lessons? Forget it."

Because it resembled a window in a house of worship, the device was called a cathedral radio, and for Charles Darwin it was indeed a kind of shrine. Hour after hour, he sat in Miss Orlova's drawing room smoking Chesterfields and listening to her Philco receiver with its mahogany cabinet and glowing dial. He especially loved the broadcasts of Arturo Toscanini conducting the NBC Symphony Orchestra. Oh, what he wouldn't give to have Emma sitting by his side, holding his hand while Mozart, Bach, and Haydn transported them to an acoustic paradise.

His present physiognomy would give her pause, of course, but not for long. She hadn't married him for his looks. With his deep-set eyes and prominent brow ridge, his former self had arguably resembled the great apes from whose evolutionary history humankind had long ago diverged. He also felt confident Emma would have encouraged him to collaborate with Miss Orlova in creating a scientifically literate horror movie. True, Emma had never warmed to his materialist understanding of the universe, and yet he could practically hear her saying, "You've been resurrected for a purpose, Charles."

Even more than the Toscanini concerts, he loved *University of Chicago Round Table*, which every Sunday brought several sages together to debate some scientific question. Was light a particle or a wave? Was there intelligent life elsewhere in the Milky Way? Might people one day travel in rocketships to Mars and Venus?

The previous week's broadcast had concerned the emerging science of genetics. It was all news—thrilling news—to Charles. The sages recounted how, extrapolating from his work with pea plants in the previous century, Friar Gregor Mendel had demonstrated that an organism's germ cells—its pollen, macrogametes, sperm, or ova—led lives quite independent of its somatic cells. Subtle was the mechanism by which successive generations went parading past Nature's reviewing stand, the observable variations tracing to discrete units of transmission called genes. Much to Charles's satisfaction, one of the sages, Professor J.B.S. Haldane, declared that evolutionary biology was "headed toward a grand synthesis of Darwinian natural selection and Mendelian genetics."

Tonight's broadcast began with the Jesuit paleontologist Teilhard de Chardin presenting the fossil skull of

Sinanthropus pekinensis, Peking Man, which he and his associates had found in 1929 in the Choukoutien cave system. Sir Arthur Keith shifted the conversation to an earlier find, the provocative skull fragments retrieved in 1912 from a gravel pit near Piltdown. "Clearly a transitional creature," he insisted, "having the jaw of an ape and the large brain pan of the modern white race."

There was something fishy about Piltdown Man, Charles decided. An authentic man-ape would surely have a *small* brain—but also erect posture and impressive manual dexterity. "Birds don't fly because they have wings," he remembered telling his eldest daughter, Annie. "Birds have wings because they fly. People don't think because they have big brains. People have big brains because they think. First comes the necessity, then the facility."

Now the anatomist Raymond Dart produced his own discovery, the famous Taung fossil from South Africa. Here was a true man-ape, Dart argued, small of brain yet upright of carriage and deft of hand—or so he inferred from the cranial aperture through which the spinal cord had descended.

"And what name did you give to your remarkable find?" asked Teilhard.

"*Australopithecus africanus,*" said Dart. "The Southern Ape of Africa. I would estimate this baby girl died two and a half million years ago."

Never turn a horror film into a science lesson, Homer had warned her. The kids won't like it. And yet the thought of writing an authentically Darwinian monster movie was starting to consume Sonya's every waking hour.

"Monster movie?" she said to her friends. "No, this must be a whole *series* of monster movies, an entire *cycle* of celluloid Trojan horses smuggling momentous ideas into young minds."

"How florid," said Homer.

"Florid is fine, but lurid is better," noted Celeste.

And then one evening, driving home from the final day's shoot on *Evil of Nocturnia*, Sonya got her idea for *The Ape Woman*. Brain throbbing, heart pounding, she sought out Mr. Darwin in the drawing room, where he was listening to Toscanini.

Much to her relief, he found her premise captivating, so they spent the next two weeks composing first a five-page treatment and then a complete screenplay. Homer and Celeste dropped in regularly to read embryonic scenes and suggest improvements. While Sonya supplied the plot turns, Mr. Darwin crafted the dialogue, most of it too elevated for this sort of nonsense, but they could always fix that in the rewrites.

—

Shortly after midnight, a radiant rock lands outside the Primate House at the Santa Monica Zoo, an event observed by Pongowana, an adult female gorilla. The uncanny meteorite blesses the ape with extraordinary intellect and the power of speech.

For several weeks Pongowana keeps her gift to herself, furtively mastering English by eavesdropping on the zoo visitors' conversations, and then one day she casually informs her keeper, a buffoon named Brisbane, "By the way, I can talk."

"Good Lord!"

"Which means you're now morally obligated to open my cage door."

"I must be losing my mind!"

After Brisbane frees Pongowana, she flees into the city. No sooner has the gorilla entered a diner on Wilshire Boulevard than the owner tells her, "We don't serve your kind here."

A dejected Pongowana descends into the LA demimonde with its dive bars, gambling dens, and cat houses. Her analytic brilliance brings her success at the poker table until a croupier banishes her for supposedly cheating.

Next she makes her way to a bordello, where the broadminded madam offers her employment, but Pongowana never becomes a favorite, and one client calls her a "dirty baboon." She then assumes a new identity, Gilda the Glissando Gorilla. A well-meaning impresario hires her to sing torch songs in his café but cancels her contract after the patrons bombard her with fruit.

—

When Sonya told Mr. Darwin he was "born to play Pongowana," he protested that his acting skills were not equal to the gorilla's ornate speeches.

"I'll deliver your lines off camera while you move your

lips in tandem with my performance," Sonya explained. "During post-production, we'll scrub my cues from the soundtrack and I'll dub in all your dialogue."

"Most ingenious," said Homer, "but wouldn't it be simpler if you just put on a gorilla suit?"

"What's going to *make* this series is Pongowana's screen presence. Audiences will know it's a gorilla, but they'll wonder how even the world's smartest ape could play the part with such finesse. The effect will be sheer magic."

"We need a stage name for Mr. Darwin," noted Celeste.

"Anything but Zolgar," he said.

"We'll call you … Ungagi the Great," said Sonya.

"I like that," said Mr. Darwin.

"I would cast Chester Conklin as Brisbane," said Homer.

"He needs a girlfriend," said Celeste. "Know what I mean?"

—

Pongowana flees to an abandoned chalet in the San Gabriel Mountains. After converting the attic into a laboratory, she tries to distill a drug that will give her what she most desires: a human form. She starts thinking of herself as Doctor Pongowana, destined to astound the world with her scientific genius.

One night, amidst a welter of burbling flasks and seething retorts, the ape concocts and drinks her elixir. Alas, the serum transforms her not into a normal woman but … a fanged, devil-eyed, beetle-browed, humanoid monster!

"Finally I, Korgora, am rid of that sniveling gorilla!" she cries. "Watch out, world! Lucifer's bride is loose!"

The Ape Woman resolves to punish all those who tormented her. She begins her project by breaking into the Wilshire Boulevard diner at closing time. "Pongowana might be ugly," she tells the owner while strangling him, "but she deserved better from you!"

"It's your most brilliant creation ever," said Homer on first seeing Sonya's Korgora make-up, which she'd wrought from yak hair, vulcanized rubber, and collodion. "A Neanderthal with sex appeal."

"It's as gruesome and tasteless as anything in *The Island of Lost Souls*," said Mr. Darwin. "The kids—is that the word?—the kids will love it."

"If not the girlfriend," said Celeste, "maybe I could play one of the hookers."

The Ape Woman retreats to her chalet, where she drinks a bottle of schnapps and falls asleep. At dawn she reverts to her fully simian self. Dr. Pongowana vaguely remembers her recent crime, and she hopes and prays her Korgora side will remain dormant forever.

Isolating herself in her lab, the gorilla resumes her quest to acquire human form. One night her true self again loses control, and she turns into Korgora. The monster descends into the city and throttles the croupier who banished her. Before the Ape Woman leaves the gambling den, she turns back into Pongowana and, horrified, beholds her victim's corpse.

Convinced now that Korgora will keep emerging unbidden, Pongowana solicits the aid of a San Francisco anthropologist. After adjusting to the strangeness of conversing with a gorilla, Dr. Xenakis advises her that, before seeking a cure for her Korgora syndrome, she should learn all she can about the history of Homo sapiens.

"Many people think evolution means modern humans descended from the apes we see around us today," says Xenakis. "But in fact contemporary gorillas, orangutans, baboons, and humans all share an extinct common ancestor." He then displays replicas of fossil skulls: Peking Man, Java Man, Neanderthal Man. While none qualifies as a true transitional species, Xenakis explains, a recent discovery, Australopithecus, testifies to the existence of a man-ape that arose in Africa millions of years ago.

Returning to LA, the gorilla again undergoes a transformation. Korgora heads for the bordello and tracks down out the client who insulted her. "Pongowana may be pathetic," she cries, cornering her intended victim, "but she's not a dirty baboon!"

Not long after the Ape Woman commits murder number three, the police arrive and drag her off to prison. The last scene plays out on the scaffold. Korgora is about to be hanged when her gorilla self emerges. While the authorities debate the morality of executing "a creature without a moral compass," Pongowana escapes. For the moment, at least, she has survived, but so has the monster. Fade-out. End credits.

Homer kissed Sonya's cheek. "The Xenakis scene is perfectly structured. Just when his lecture is getting boring, he pulls out skulls."

"And right after we've scratched our heads over '*Australopithecus*,' we get a juicy murder," said Celeste.

"Might we have Xenakis talk about the *engine* behind evolution?" asked Mr. Darwin. "Wouldn't it be marvelous to make a movie in which a major character says 'natural selection'?"

"Not if nobody comes to see it," said Homer.

"Let's save 'natural selection' for *The Ape Woman Returns*," said Sonya. "After which, of course, we'll do *The Ape Woman Strikes Back* followed by *The Ape Woman Joins the Foreign Legion*, *The Ape Woman at the Folies Bergère*, *The Ape Woman Meets the Sheik of Araby*—on and on, forever!"

Isaac Bachman was in low spirits, his despair bordering on despondency, when Miss Bressler handed him a screenplay titled *The Ape Woman*. He'd spent the afternoon pondering the recent box-office performance, or lack thereof, of the Excelsior franchises, including the Clint Sterling westerns, the Limehouse Larry mysteries, and the Pirate Jenny swashbucklers. Even Miss Orlova's potboilers no longer brought in boffo-size bucks—and yet here was a script she'd written with somebody called Carlos Doran.

The title sounded promising, so he locked the office door and poured a glass of scotch. The first scene, about a weird rock from outer space, was ridiculous but gripping, and the episodes set in a "private gentleman's club" were delectably risqué, and the damn thing kept getting better and better. Miss Orlova had written a hell of a part for herself, a brainy gorilla who periodically became a half-human monster, though he wasn't sure the actress could manage the heavy harnesses she'd need to play the ape.

From his late father Isaac had received a priceless nugget of wisdom: "A man's worst enemy is his better judgment." So far Sol Bachman's maxim had served his firstborn well. Isaac's better judgment had told him not to leave the Garment District and head for Hollywood, and yet it had all worked out. His better judgment had told him not to hire an unknown to play his lady vampire, but he did, and the rest was history.

"Against my better judgment, I'm giving this Korgora thing the green light," he told Miss Orlova upon summoning her to his office.

She offered him a wide Nocturnia grin.

"Who the hell is Carlos Doran?" asked Isaac.

"My alter ego."

Isaac ran a finger along his bronze Apollo statuette, his only industry award. Somehow Ben Winkleberg, Excelsior's Chairman of the Board in New York, had convinced his fellow executives that Isaac deserved special recognition for producing a lucrative farce called *The Uptown Urchins* and its equally profitable sequels, *Uptown Urchins on Broadway* and *Uptown Urchins Meet the Brooklyn Dodgers*.

"There are too many sets," said Isaac. "We can't afford all these speaking parts. And yet, take me to the nuthouse, lock me up in Bedlam, we're going to shoot *The Ape Woman* the way you wrote it."

"Wonderful."

"Well, not *exactly* the way you wrote it. The science speeches have to go. Nobody wants to hear about fossils and extinction and Austrian pithegrams."

"But that's the educational heart of the film."

"This is a fucking *horror movie*, Sonya. It doesn't *have* an educational heart."

Steeling herself, Miss Orlova looked him in the eye and said, "Did I tell you Zukor wants to know when my Excelsior contract expires?"

"His company's on the skids," said Isaac in a dismissive tone.

"So is every other studio in town. Zukor thinks I can improve morale at Paramount just by walking through the gates."

"Fuck Zukor. Okay, keep the lectures—but take out the Latin."

"No Latin, no Ape Woman. This is going to be *big*, Isaac. It so happens we can hire the gorilla for next to nothing. My brother saved his life, and the owner is eternally grateful."

"You're imagining a male gorilla in a female role? We'll have to keep his schlong off camera."

"Lionel Atwill is eager to play Xenakis, and Chester Conklin has agreed to do Brisbane."

"Since when did you become a producer?"

"Just trying to make your job easier."

"Do me a favor and stop doing me favors."

"So who should direct?" said Miss Orlova.

"Not Ferris?"

"Let's hire Lamprecht away from Monogram. Those German refugees can do genius on a budget."

In collaboration with Homer, Celeste, and Mr. Darwin, Sonya cranked out two more drafts, and *The Ape Woman* went into production, Klaus Lamprecht at the helm. The German refugee brought cinematographic panache to the seedy café, smoky gambling den, and gilded bordello, each atmospheric set designed by Herman Geisler, master of making bricks without straw. Cast as a prostitute, Celeste acquitted herself well, nailing every line on the first take. Lamprecht couldn't believe how beautifully Ungagi the Great took directions, down to moving his lips as Sonya, stationed just out of camera range, delivered Pongowana's dialogue.

Later that week she put on the yak hair, and Lamprecht shot her murdering the croupier and the bordello client. The next day they filmed the Ape Woman escaping the noose and Xenakis holding forth about extinct common ancestors. Thenceforth the cast and crew burned through the script at the rate of five pages a day, and suddenly it was in the can, the whole enchilada.

As *The Ape Woman* went through post-production—cutting, looping, scoring, opticals—Sonya realized that her house guest had become not only her muse but also an object of desire. The raw animal fact of Mr. Darwin had stirred within her some secret beast, her innermost Edwina Hyde. Falling asleep each night, she imagined him rushing into her bedchamber, his male organ descending from his loins like landing gear from a fuselage. Occasionally she placed her boyfriend in the scene, a *menagerie-à-trois*. Of course, she could imagine no actual such arrangement that would leave intact the good thing she had going with Homer, but who could say what the future might bring?

The critical reception accorded *The Ape Woman* exceeded Sonya's wildest expectations. "This simian thriller provides frights, frissons, and dollops of philosophy," *Daily Variety* declared, "just as it will surely provide Excelsior Pictures with handsome profits."

"This time out, the Woman of a Thousand Faces shares the screen with a trained gorilla called Ungagi the Great, cast as a brilliant and verbose female ape, Dr. Pongowana," the *Hollywood Reporter* noted. "Impressively, Miss Orlova, who plays Korgora, the monster spawned by Pongowana's Jekyll-to-Hyde experiments, never allows her hairy co-star to upstage her."

"Hollywood should be grateful that so many of the UFA artisans who fled Hitler came to our town," the *Los Angeles Times* review began, "because now even shoddy efforts like *The Ape Woman* boast the ineffable enchantments of German Expressionism." Much to his credit, and probably over the editor's objections, the critic had titled his piece "Australopithecinema."

Throughout the first month following its release, Sonya surreptitiously attended *Ape Woman* screenings. When the lights came up, she always sought out adolescent moviegoers. "What did you make of those fossil skulls?" she would ask. "Did you follow the stuff Xenakis was spouting about human descent?" Usually she got blank stares, but occasionally a boy or girl would mutter something about extinct common ancestors.

Three weeks into its release, a crisis befell the picture. Having learned that it endorsed the simian theory of human origins, Nigel and Desmond started a campaign to have *The Ape Woman* banned in Tennessee, Mississippi, and Arkansas, the states that had already exiled Darwin from the biology curriculum. The brothers knew they wouldn't run afoul of the First Amendment, as the Supreme Court had long ago ruled, in *Mutual Film Corporation v. Industrial Commission of Ohio*, that motion pictures weren't protected speech. And yet things didn't work out as the Rowens had planned. Although the state legislatures had gleefully passed prohibition bills, and the governors had reflexively signed them, the collateral publicity increased attendance in New England and the mid-Atlantic states. And while *The Ape Woman* never yielded the "handsome profits" predicted by *Daily Variety*, it performed well enough to merit a sequel.

"We would've done even *better* if you'd taken out the Austrian pithegrams," Mr. Bachman told Sonya. "That said, if you insist on shoehorning science lessons into the next one, I won't try to stop you."

On the first morning in April, Sonya and the rest of the Simian Cinema Scribbling Committee gathered in the library to discuss the box-office catastrophe the Rowens had nearly caused in the South and to knock around ideas for *The Ape Woman Returns*. Although it was April Fool's Day, neither Homer nor Celeste was in a mischievous mood, and Mr. Darwin looked positively morose.

"Let me share some sad discoveries," he said after everyone was seated at a table overspread with pastries and fruit. Moving on slipper-shod feet and hairy knuckles, he approached a glass-doored bookcase. "I've been spending my Sundays haunting flea markets and used-book shops, looking for specimens of that troublesome beast, the American biology textbook."

"I always accompany him," said Celeste. "It's shocking how many retailers won't do business with gorillas."

Mr. Darwin returned to the table with four volumes in his clutches. "Here's the one that put John Scopes in the dock." He flourished *A Civic Biology: Presented in Problems*. "George Hunter's 1914 bestseller contains the chapter Scopes assigned his students." He held up *New Civic Biology*. "Shortly after the trial, the publisher shrewdly changed the title and cut out all serious consideration of human descent. The book still sells in big numbers."

Radiating distress, Mr. Darwin ate a half-dozen slices of cantaloupe, lit a cigarette, and displayed Truman Moon's *Biology for Beginners*. "The pre-Scopes edition called evolution 'the central idea in biology' and featured my portrait as the frontispiece." He brandished a later edition. "For the post-Scopes version of 1926, the publisher replaced dozens of pages about the unity of life with a short chapter called 'The Hypothesis of Racial Development' and changed the frontispiece to an illustration of a human stomach." The scientist took a drag on his Chesterfield. "Promise me something, dear friends. The term 'natural selection' will figure in *The Ape Woman Returns*—okay?"

The commitment proved easy to keep. Act One featured the usual melodramatic folderol, notably Korgora destroying Dr. Pongowana's laboratory so she could never concoct a serum for suppressing her alter ego. But Act Two found Pongowana, determined as always to understand her origins, consulting the elderly Dr. Rangorst, who inhabits underground chambers adjacent to the Los Angeles sewers. Rangorst was barely out of adolescence when he'd begun creating outlandish reptiles. "Nature furnished me with accidental novelties," he tells Pongowana, "and I took it from there, determining who would mate with whom, generation upon generation. Here in my hidden world I have replaced the undirected mechanism Darwin called natural selection with the techniques developed by dog breeders and pigeon fanciers."

"George Zucco would be great in this part," said Sonya.

"Could we amend Rangorst's line?" said Mr. Darwin. "'I have replaced the nonteleological mechanism that Darwin called—'"

"Surely you're joking," said Sonya.

Over the course of seven decades Rangorst has produced a caiman with serrated spikes on its tail, a snake with rudimentary forelegs, and an iguana as large as a canoe. "Just as my conscious and deliberate choices have modified existing species within my lifetime," he explains, "so have mindless environmental pressures transmuted our planet's plants and animals over millions of years."

Having learned that trying to ban a movie will only make people want to see it, Nigel and Desmond ignored the release of *The Ape Woman Returns*. Even without the publicity the brothers had accorded the original Korgora, the sequel did brisk business, and it marked the emergence of Ungagi the Great as the most popular nonhuman star since Rin Tin Tin. From sea to shining sea, Ungagi fan clubs, stuffed animals, and comic books proliferated. Mr. Bachman straightway commissioned a third Ape Woman script, hinting that it might be Excelsior's first Trucolor feature.

Writing *The Ape Woman Strikes Back* with Sonya, Homer, and Celeste provided Mr. Darwin with his most gratifying Hollywood experience thus far, since the Scribbling Committee managed to get "reproductive fitness" into the mouths of three different scientists. "Because Nature is so prolific, creatures find themselves competing with each other for limited living space and food supplies," the herpetologist elaborated. "In the struggle for existence, the individual with advantageous characteristics is more likely than its fellows to reach sexual maturity and pass those traits on to the next generation."

"I think we've picked the wrong title for the third Korgora," said Sonya. "We should call it *The Ape Woman Reaches Sexual Maturity*."

"Miss Orlova, forgive me if I don't always grasp when

you're being facetious," said Mr. Darwin. "Remember, we're from different centuries."

"That was indeed a joke, sir. The ideal title would be *Forbidden Desires of the Nymphomaniacal Ape Woman*."

Although Isaac Bachman ultimately decided not to shoot the film in Trucolor, *The Ape Woman Strikes Back* found an audience, cleared a $95,000 profit, and enhanced Ungagi's popularity. *Spawn of the Ape Woman* also recouped its costs and then some, as did *The Ape Woman Meets the Blood Demon*. By contrast, *Curse of the Ape Woman* never got to show its box-office mettle, owing to an abrupt reversal in the fortunes of Excelsior Pictures.

Sonya learned about the disaster on the first day of shooting: a laboratory scene, Pongowana having built a new one following Korgora's rampage in *The Ape Woman Returns*. During Sonya's lunch break, Eddie the errand boy brought her a note from Mr. Bachman. *Report to me pronto.*

No sooner had Sonya entered Isaac's office than her heart sank. Sprawled across the Naugahyde couch, sipping coffee and grinning like hyenas, were the Rowen brothers.

"They insisted on being here when I told you the bad news," said Isaac, sucking on a pipe he'd forgotten to light.

"Except *we're* going to tell her the bad news," said Nigel.

"Which is actually *good* news," added Desmond.

"While you were making your monkey pictures, Miss Orlova, Desmond and I were looking into Excelsior's finances. We discovered that on three separate occasions the company missed a payment on its five-hundred-thousand-dollar loan from Bank of America."

"Being magnanimous souls," said Desmond, "we contacted the Excelsior comptroller and arranged to assume the debt."

"Jubilee has been flourishing," Nigel explained. "Beyond Texas, we've cornered the market in Georgia, Arizona, and South Carolina."

"After scrubbing acres of red ink from Excelsior's books," said Desmond, "we purchased the lion's share of its publicly traded stock."

Sonya's jaw dropped as far as the hinge allowed. "So you bozos now own Excelsior?"

"No, we bozos now own Epiphany Studios," said Nigel. "Excelsior no long exists. The Board of Directors is happy with the new identity, since they get to keep their jobs."

"And Isaac and I don't?" said Sonya.

"You and most other Excelsior personnel are about to become familiar faces around the employment agency," said Desmond.

"Grant Ferris is coming to work for us," said Nigel. "He never forgave you for replacing him with Lamprecht. We won't be making horror pictures, of course. Epiphany will give the world only edifying entertainment."

Isaac lifted the bronze Apollo from his desk and brought it protectively to his chest. "So you're closing down *Curse of the Ape Woman*?"

"We'll take care of dismantling the sets," said

Desmond. "That will teach you, Miss Orlova, to steal heirlooms from us."

"Heirlooms?" said Isaac.

"Charles Darwin's right cortical hemisphere," Nigel explained.

"I don't understand," said Isaac.

"We've seen all five Ape Woman movies," said Desmond. "Was that our dear Celeste playing the trollop in the first one? We thought she was excellent."

"I can't wait to tell her," said Sonya drily.

"Mr. Darwin *also* has a promising Hollywood career ahead of him," said Nigel. "He's much better at portraying apes than theorizing about them. We assume your brother installed his other hemisphere."

"Indeed," said Sonya.

"I wish I knew what the hell you're talking about," said Isaac.

"Too bad every single Ape Woman movie is about to vanish," said Desmond. "Camera negatives, interpositives, release prints. Apart from some ill-conceived and pedantic dialogue, we found those pictures quite amusing."

"What do you mean 'vanish'?" asked Isaac.

"Mr. Ferris has a poetic way of putting it," said Nigel. "'A movie is a fragile thing. Silver nitrate burns. Celluloid melts. An entire series may disappear overnight, leaving behind only a fistful of production stills and a few strips of 35mm magic littering the cutting-room floor.'"

CHAPTER 4
THE EMPEROR OF ASPIRATION

She wept, she raged, she gnashed her teeth. She considered, half seriously, visiting the Rowens wearing her Ape Woman make-up and chopping up their textbooks with an ax. Although the fall of Excelsior did not necessary portend the end of her acting career, Sonya feared that her best Hollywood years were now behind her —and, indeed, when she telephoned Adolph Zukor and asked if he still wanted her in Paramount's roster of stars, he replied, drily, "My interest in Sonya Orlova has waned since she began making those egghead gorilla movies, which weren't exactly box-office smashes."

Throughout the following week she and Mr. Bachman worked frantically to salvage the franchise. When they offered *Curse of the Ape Woman* to George Shaefer at RKO, he rolled his eyes and said, "I've got my hands full with Orson Welles right now, and a five-hundred-pound gorilla won't make my life easier."

They had no better luck with Herbert Yates at Republic.

"Sorry, Isaac and Sonya. Unless it's a horse opera, I can't take a chance on it."

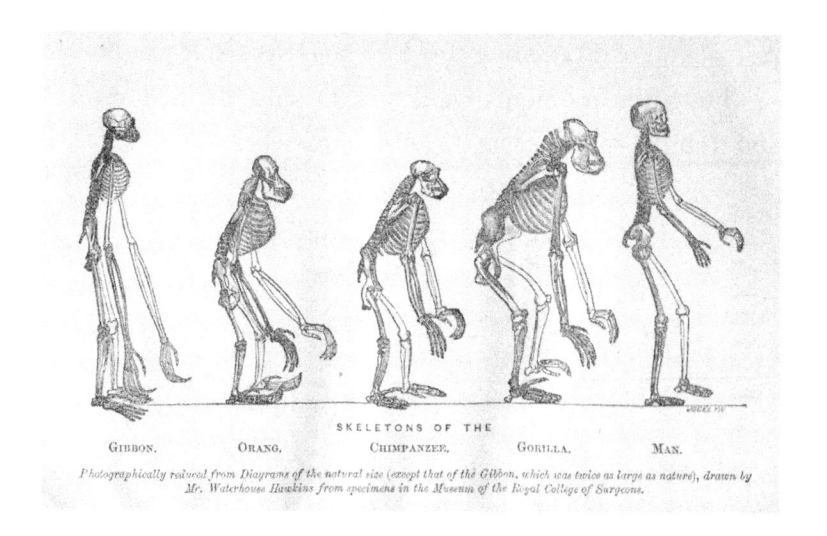

SKELETONS OF THE
GIBBON. ORANG. CHIMPANZEE. GORILLA. MAN.

Photographically reduced from Diagrams of the natural size (except that of the Gibbon, which was twice as large as nature), drawn by Mr. Waterhouse Hawkins from specimens in the Museum of the Royal College of Surgeons.

Sigmund Neufeld at Producers Releasing Corporation also showed them the door. "You think I don't know about all the evolution *mishegaas* in your monkey pictures? I have enough enemies these days without I should get in trouble with God."

As for Sam Katzman at Monogram, he sneered at Isaac and remarked, "Have you forgotten how you hired Lamprecht away from me?"

Faced with the task of telling her friends that the Ape Woman was on the verge of extinction, Sonya procrastinated until Sunday morning, when she convened a Scribbling Committee meeting in the library, ostensibly to pick apart the first draft of *Wrath of the Ape Woman*. She cleared her throat, set her palm on the script, and, as Homer, Celeste, and Mr. Darwin listened with ever increasing dismay, told them the whole story: the assumption of Excelsior's Bank of America debt by the Rowens, the manipulation of the company's stock, the threatened destruction of all existing Korgora negatives and prints.

"From the moment Nigel and Desmond hired me as God's shill," said Celeste, "I knew they were snakes."

"So my beloved doppelgänger, Dr. Pongowana, has gone to her reward." Mr. Darwin indeed looked like an ape in mourning. "I guess Jubilee gets the last laugh."

"Maybe we could peddle *Curse of the Ape Woman* and this new one to Katzman at Monogram," said Homer, "or Shaefer at RKO, or Yates at—"

"We tried all that," said Sonya.

Homer exhaled in slow motion. "Well, then it's checkmate."

Because Sonya's mind rarely stopped racing, she was not surprised when a big idea now blossomed in her brain. "Check? Yes. Mate? I'm not so sure." She bit into a bagel. "I keep going back to the humiliation the Rowens suffered after they got *The Ape Woman* banned in three states."

"They lost that battle—but now they've won the war," said Homer.

"Okay, but what if the Rowens encountered a crowd-pleasing movie they found so appalling that they felt compelled to attack it ten times more vehemently than they did *The Ape Woman*?"

"They'd receive ten times the public vilification," said Celeste, perking up.

"Exactly," said Sonya.

"Maybe," said Homer.

"And I'm not talking about another potboiler," said Sonya, nodding. "This will be a by-God prestige picture, dripping with class. If the Rowens start railing against it, the backlash could put them out of business."

"Or there might not be a backlash at all," said Homer. "A movie that outrages the Rowens will probably outrage a *lot* of people."

"But *more* people would like to see the First Amendment finally come to Hollywood. The time is ripe. Everybody used to treat the Production Code like it was the Law of Moses, but today we're seeing cracks in the tablets. The Code outlaws swear words, but last year Gable said 'damn' in *Gone with the Wind*, and audiences ate it up. The Code demands deference to religion, but even as we speak, MGM is filming the Broadway hit *Susan and God*, featuring Joan Crawford as a pious busybody."

"Of course, before the Rowens try to ban our movie," said Homer, "we'll have to get around to making it."

"That might be simpler than it sounds," said Celeste.

"Oh?" said the other Committee members in unison.

"Do you know about your brother's windfall?" Celeste asked Sonya.

"Windfall? The last I heard from Vasily was a Christmas card he forgot to sign."

"Maybe I shouldn't be telling you this, but Dr. Orlov was recently paid two million dollars by some Egyptian king—"

"Farouk?" said Homer.

"That's the one," said Celeste. "King Farouk."

"Two million?" said Sonya.

"He removed a brain tumor from the king's three-year-old daughter, an operation no licensed surgeon would attempt, since Farouk would've had 'em executed if it failed. The princess is doing fine."

"This all savors of a Dickensian plot contrivance," said Mr. Darwin

"If it's a contrivance," said Celeste, "it was authored by Providence, not a Victorian novelist."

"Unless God *is* a Victorian novelist," said Homer.

"So what sort of film would expose the Rowens as philistines bent on dragging America back into the nineteenth century?" asked Sonya.

"Let's adapt something by the Marquis de Sade," suggested Mr. Darwin, grinning apishly.

"Remember our festival of evolution movies?" said Homer. "It began with the most blasphemous picture ever made in Hollywood—Charles Laughton as God the Cosmic Torturer, whose creatures know they'll experience unimaginable agony if they don't worship him properly."

"Whereas if they *do* worship him properly, they'll also experience unimaginable agony," added Mr. Darwin evenly.

"Yes!" cried Sonya. "That's it! We'll bait the trap with a brand-new *Island of Dr. Moreau*. Not a garden-variety remake, but a Technicolor, star-studded, three million dollar—"

"Two million," Celeste corrected her.

"Two-million-dollar extravaganza featuring Sonya Orlova as Mr. Wells's mad scientist."

"What makes you imagine he'd sell us the rights?" asked Homer. "He hated the Laughton version."

"Once he learns we're making the film to mortify the enemies of his old teacher, Thomas Huxley, he'll surely join our side."

"Let's not underestimate the Rowens," said Homer. "They're too smart to fall for this sort of ploy."

"Oh, they'll fall all right," said Sonya. "You see, in our loose adaptation, Dr. Moreau will be visited by two flimflam artists, Nigel and Desmond ... er, Neville and Derek

Rowen—*Bowen*—whose paleontologist grandfather knew and despised Charles Darwin."

"And the idea of seeing satiric versions of themselves up on the big screen will drive our boys around the bend?" said Homer. "Is that it?"

"They'll lose their minds," said Sonya confidently.

"They'll flip their lids," said Celeste.

"I love it," said Homer.

"And Jubilee Publishing will never be the same," said Sonya.

She spent every waking hour of the next two weeks working on her adaptation of *The Island of Dr. Moreau*, running the embryonic scenes past the rest of the Scribbling Committee and assimilating their better suggestions. At one point Celeste proposed that the movie should be a musical, and this preposterous idea gradually grew on Sonya, inspiring her to include tentative lyrics in the subsequent three drafts.

In bending the novel to her purposes, Sonya gave Dr. Moreau's domain a name, Desolation Isle, and replaced the alcoholic assistant, Montgomery, with a far more appealing character, Dr. Rivard, who would ultimately emerge as the film's hero. She also eliminated the distasteful element of vivisection, a matter of making the two physicians know about opium-based anesthetics. Instead of reliving their surgical ordeals in the House of Pain, Moreau's misbegotten hybrids—her boar-puma, ox-lemur, bison-marmoset, and so on—would nurture hopes of returning to the Palace of Rapture and experiencing additional ecstatic pipe dreams.

"Do we really want to put opium in a family picture?" asked Celeste.

"*The Wizard of Oz* paved the way," said Sonya. "Remember the poppies?"

—

Although he has been Dr. Moreau's acolyte for years, one morning Dr. Rivard wakes up realizing he can no longer assist in the creation of monstrosities. (Cue "First Do No Harm," sung by Rivard.)

When Moreau acquires a panther he intends to "mold into a human female," Rivard finds the idea so outrageous he flees the fortress compound. In the jungle he encounters the dystopian community of the Beast People. The Sayer of the Law, a jackal-baboon chimera, inducts new members by requiring them to chant a parody of the Ten Commandments. (Cue "That Is the Law," sung by the hybrids.)

The Sayer helps Rivard build a raft. While crossing to an adjacent landmass, Aspiration Isle, Rivard resolves to make benevolent use of the surgical techniques he learned from Moreau.

—

For the chant lyrics, Sonya simply lifted Wells's text word for word. "Not to go on all fours—that is the Law.

Are we not men? Not to suck up drink—that is the Law. Are we not men? Not to eat fish or flesh—that is the Law. Are we not men?" The refrain departed only slightly from the original. "Hers is the hand that makes. Hers is the knife that shapes. Hers is the Palace of Rapture."

Lured by rumors, anguished misfits begin arriving at Rivard's clinic, all of them haunted by an overwhelming sense of having been born into the wrong species. (Cue "I Must Sing to the Moon," performed by Amelia, an aspiring wolf.)

Each misfit happily enters the surgical theater, eager to acquire the outward appearance of a wolf, fox, bear, tiger, goat, or hyena. Among the patients is Rufus Jones, a young would-be ape who will become the Gorilla Man. (Latter part to be played by Ungagi the Great.)

Following their transformations, most Fur Folk ask to remain in this fragile paradise, knowing the outside world will perceive them as repulsive freaks. Rivard assents, but he invites them to regard themselves as threads in the vast life-web that envelops the planet. The ties that bind them to the other species on Aspiration—the butterflies, beetles, crabs, parrots, and tortoises—are as real as a monsoon. (Cue "Ten Million Fruits on the Tree of Life," sung by Rivard.)

The surgeon goes so far as to teach the Fur Folk a variant of the Beast People's catechism. "Not to confuse natural selection with divine intervention—that is the Law. Are we not animals? Not to call ourselves the apex of creation—that is the Law. Are we not animals? Not to deny extinct common ancestors—that is the Law. Are we not animals?"

The subsequent chorus celebrates the twin evolutionary imperatives of sex and annihilation. "Lust is the hand that makes. Death is the tool that shapes. Loss is the scythe that winnows. Passion is the power that provides."

―

While impressed by Sonya's audacity, Homer and Celeste insisted that, if the group really wanted this to be a family picture, they must omit the encomiums to lust and death. Yes, *The Wizard of Oz* had its opium scene, but the movie didn't get audiences thinking about fucking and oblivion. Sonya promised her friends she would take their critique to heart.

―

The plot thickens when two confidence men, Neville and Derek Bowen, are shipwrecked on Desolation. After witnessing the Beast People recite their servile chant, they are apprehended by Moreau's guards. Having turned his panther into a creature called Leita, Moreau now expects her to mate with the Bowen of her choice. If their union results in viable offspring, the scientist will declare herself a deity. (Cue "I Have the Urge to Be a Demiurge," sung by Moreau.)

The brothers are naturally appalled. After freeing Leita from the fortress compound, they seek out the Sayer of the Law, who transports Leita and the Bowens to the safety of Aspiration Isle.

Meeting for the first time, the Panther Woman and Rivard fall head over heels.

Gradually Neville and Derek come to appreciate the compassion that guides Rivard's scalpel, and they conceive a plan to topple Moreau. Phase one has the Fur Folk crossing to Desolation on improvised rafts. When the Beast People scorn the immigrants as despicable invaders, Leita shames them with a song. (Cue "There Is No Normal, Only Love.")

Allies now, the two tribes besiege the fortress compound. Moreau's guards are no match for the fanged, clawed, taloned army at the gates. As Moreau's domain goes up in flames, she flees and is swallowed by quicksand.

In the dénouement the Beast People and the Fur Folk mourn their fallen comrades, while the Bowen brothers vow to abstain from confidence games. A double wedding ensues. After Neville takes the Wolf Woman as his wife, the saintly Rivard and the sultry Panther Woman trade marriage vows. (Cue "The Southern Cross Will Guide Us Home.") Fade-out. End credits.

Everyone agreed *The Island of Dr. Moreau* was too solemn a title for so ebullient a movie, so Sonya changed it to *The Emperor of Aspiration* (an epithet for Dr. Rivard). After Mrs. Blackwood finished typing the latest draft, Sonya grabbed a carbon copy and drove out to the Orlov Clinic. She found Vasily in the turret, putting on a surgical gown.

Assisted by both nurses, he freed up the anesthetized patient's scalp, pulled it down over his face like a veil, incised the skull, and popped off a yarmulke–size bone cap, thus releasing a torrent of blood. The abrupt drop in intracranial pressure would presumably save the patient's life.

"How long will this take?" asked Sonya.

"Shut up," said Vasily.

After cauterizing the leaking vein, he left it to Yvonne and Celeste to close up the patient. Frowning profusely, he approached Sonya, who lost no time outlining her scheme.

"Do you really expect me to squander my King Farouk jackpot on a damn horror movie?" asked Vasily.

Sonya waved the carbon copy around like a coquette fluttering a fan. "We think of it more as a South Seas romance, a kind of sequel to *Mutiny on the Bounty*."

"Except everybody ends up in a jungle paradise instead of on Pitcairn's Island," added Celeste.

"Also, our version has songs," said Sonya.

"Songs? Please, no." Vasily flicked his hand toward the script as if shooing a fly. "This isn't my sort of project."

"Have you forgotten how I helped you smuggle yourself through medical school?"

"That's a good point," piped up Yvonne.

"Tonight I'll read your script and phone you," said Vasily, "but you must understand I'm not about to invest in any goddamn South Seas musical horror movie."

Throughout his residency at Miss Orlova's mansion, Charles Darwin often yearned to see his own estate once more, Down House with its sheep meadows, woods, and greenhouses, not to mention his thinking path, the loop of crushed flint he'd walked along compulsively, week after week, month after month, until one day he arrived at a destination called the theory of natural selection—though recently he'd come to realize that the south terrace of Medusa Manor was likewise conducive to his meditations. Pacing about this congenial half-acre on the morning of the summer solstice, the 21st of June, 1940, he surveyed the goldfish pond, flower garden, birdbath, and solitary eucalyptus tree, taking perverse satisfaction in the quiet warfare raging behind these idyllic façades, for every last carp, tanager, stag beetle, and chaparral chipmunk was engaged in an unconscious, unsupervised struggle to survive long enough to bequeath its germ cells to the next generation.

Back in County Kent, he'd often wondered what it was like to be a lower lifeform. How did existence *feel* to a cat, hare, horse, or gibbon—or, for that matter, to a centipede, slug, barnacle, or dragonfly? These questions were arguably unanswerable and perhaps even absurd. If Charles were to somehow dissolve his physical and mental essence into the body and brain of a cat, he could never subsequently report on the experience, since the notion of collecting impressions for later linguistic transmission would have been, throughout his feline sojourn, an unthinkable thought.

But then came Charles's American adventure. Thanks to the Rowen brothers, he'd spent five weeks in a zone halfway between *Homo sapiens* and the pongids. His incompleteness had nearly driven him mad, and yet, even as he gave his Peripatetic Panorama performances, his human side vowed that, if he ever got his other cortical hemisphere back, he would force his reconstituted self to summon Brother Zolgar's career to mind. Alas, although he'd transitioned from the pongid world to the human without permanent psychic damage, he could dredge up almost nothing of Zolgar's consciousness. But he would keep on trying. At the very least those impressions, if recovered, would improve his performance as the Gorilla Man in Miss Orlova's adaptation of Mr. Wells's most vivid novel.

Although Charles believed *The Emperor of Aspiration* was going to be a nonsensical movie that couldn't possibly topple the Rowens' textbook empire, he intended to do everything he could to make the picture succeed. He'd never known anyone quite like Sonya Orlova, this woman of such consummate brio, passion, and *joie de vivre*. She enchanted him beyond all telling. O brave new Tinseltown, that has such creatures in it.

Thus it happened that the father of the natural-selection hypothesis spent the longest day of the year trying to conjure the wayward soul and vanished sensibility of a creature called Zolgar, while all around him a myriad vertebrates, invertebrates, and members of the vegetable kingdom went about the business of being themselves.

True to his promise, Vasily telephoned Sonya right after reading *The Emperor of Aspiration*, and his reaction sent her over the moon. Any movie made from this screenplay, he declared, would be "entertaining to a fault." His only suggestion was to cut "There Is No Normal, Only Love," which he found "so cloying it will give moviegoers diabetes."

"Those lyrics are placeholders," said Sonya. "I'm planning to hire professional songwriters."

With Vasily's fortune in her pocket, she shifted into high gear, hiring the firm of Leland and Wintergreen to incorporate her ambitions as an entity called Pinnacle Pictures, with herself as president and Vasily as vice president. After Isaac Bachman and Klaus Lamprecht expressed their enthusiasm for the script, she attached them to the project as executive producer and director respectively. Next she mailed a draft to the Rowens. Although it included the "Are we not animals?" chant, it lacked the refrain beginning "Lust is the hand," which Sonya now agreed had to come out. "I'm actually glad you boys killed the Ape Woman," her cover letter began. "As you'll see, we've gone on to bigger and better things."

Somehow Isaac got a script into the hands of H.G. Wells himself, who wrote back, "I was royally unamused by James Whale's *The Invisible Man* (which turned my rational protagonist into a lunatic) and Erle Kenton's *The Island of Lost Souls* (which sacrificed philosophy for sensationalism), and I feel confident *The Emperor of Aspiration*, with its barmy musical numbers, will be worse than either one." He then added, true to Sonya's prediction, "That said, because you're aiming to distress Nigel and Desmond Rowen, I'll sell you the rights for a pittance—my way of thumbing my nose at their grandfather, who routinely tormented my old teacher, Thomas Henry Huxley. However, you must preserve my anonymity by leaving my name off the credits and keeping the present terrible title."

Buoyed by Wells's blessing, Sonya and Isaac showed the script to the legendary team of Richard Rodgers and Lorenz Hart, who said he must be kidding. Yip Harburg and Harold Arlen, fresh off *The Wizard of Oz*, had the same reaction. Just when it looked like the picture wasn't going to be a musical after all, Bert Kalmar and Harry Ruby, who'd written witty songs for the Marx Brothers, said they'd love to try providing some catchy tunes and droll lyrics.

In what proved to be a stroke of genius, Sonya and Isaac formed a partnership with Louis B. Mayer, two million dollars being the sort of money that talked loudly and at length in Depression-era Hollywood. Mr. Mayer agreed to lease his soundstages to Pinnacle and distribute the film through Loew's, Inc. He stipulated only that the major roles must go to MGM contract players, most especially his great discovery Hedy Lamarr, who would be perfect for transmuted panther, Leita. ("The Most Beautiful Woman in the World and the Woman of a Thousand Faces, together in one terrific picture!" he enthused, testing out a possible advertising pitch on Sonya and Isaac, who pretended they thought it was fabulous.) The remaining parts were easily filled with Metro talent: Walter Pidgeon as Rivard, Wallace Beery as the Sayer of the Law, Lew Ayres and Melvyn Douglas as the Bowens.

Because Isaac had once furthered the acting ambitions of the flamboyant Hedda Hopper, routinely giving her roles in the Clint Sterling westerns and the Uptown Urchins comedies, she dutifully read the script with an eye to promoting her benefactor's movie in her syndicated gossip column. On October 14, 1940, Sonya opened the *Los Angeles Times* to find Miss Hopper perpetrating her usual inimitable mixture of puffery and falsehoods.

A forthcoming Pinnacle Pictures musical, The Emperor of Aspiration, *starring Sonya Orlova as a mad scientist and Walter Pidgeon as an altruistic surgeon, has apparently caught the attention of every Hollywood player who doesn't take himself too seriously.*

For it happens that the Orlova-penned screenplay, which I read last week and absolutely adored, features a passel of delightful animal cameos, the "Fur Folk," and you won't believe how many household names are vying for these coveted roles.

Rising star Lena Horne has already been cast as the Wolf Woman. Rumor has it Jimmy Cagney, who made us laugh as Bottom the Donkey Man in A Midsummer Night's Dream, *hopes to land a similar role in the Klaus Lamprecht-helmed spectacle, while any day now Bert Lahr expects to hear that he's going to play a Lion Man again.*

Smart money says The Emperor of Aspiration, *which finds independent producer Isaac Bachman teaming with none other than Louis B. Mayer, will be 1941's answer to MGM's hit fantasy,* The Wizard of Oz.

Thanks to Hedda Hopper's hearsay and canards, dozens of major stars were soon clamoring to become Fur Folk. James Cagney indeed wanted the Donkey Man part, and Bert Lahr's agent insisted his client simply *had* to play the Lion Man. Jimmy Durante joined the troupe as the Rhinoceros Man, W.C. Fields as the Sloth Man, and Mickey Rooney as the Goat Boy.

When it came to casting Rufus Jones, the youth Moreau transforms into the Gorilla Man (the latter to be played by her house guest hiding behind his Ungagi persona), Sonya insisted on total control, for what a lovely in-joke it would be if Rufus were a dead ringer for Charles Darwin. Her search ended when she happened to catch RKO's *They Knew What They Wanted* and noticed newcomer Karl Malden in a supporting role. The instant he saw Malden's publicity photo, Mr. Darwin remarked, "Yes, that's the face I used to see in the mirror when I shaved, bulbous nose and all!"

Although neither Sonya nor Isaac believed in Providence, when they considered how few crises had plagued the filming of *The Emperor of Aspiration*, they couldn't help imagining that a benevolent higher power wanted to see this offbeat extravaganza up on the screen. True, the script had its blasphemous moments, but Sonya accepted Isaac's conclusion that, if God existed, He surely had a sense of humor. "The halls of any heaven worthy of the name," Isaac insisted, "ring with laughter as well as psalms."

Apart from Providence, the efficiency of the *Aspiration* shoot doubtless traced to Sonya and Isaac's decision to film most scenes under the predictable conditions of the MGM soundstages. For the establishing shots of Desolation and Aspiration, the second unit director exploited Santa Miguel Island, easily reached from Ventura by steam launch. Thanks to that marvelous special effect called stunt doubles, none of the *Aspiration* actors had to cross the strait, with the exception of Celeste, cast as Moreau's servant M'ling, a malamute-meerkat hybrid who paced the shores of Desolation longing aloud for a better life.

While Klaus Lamprecht worked on getting chemistry into the moments between Rivard and Leita, and drama into the confrontations between Moreau and the Bowens, Sonya and Isaac supervised the construction of the fortress compound. Shortly after the completion of principal photography, the assistant director rounded up the Fur Folk's stand-ins, plus the generally obscure actors playing the Beast People (with Isaac's cousin Max doubling for Wallace Beery, the Sayer of the Law), and herded them onto the MGM back lot. For three days the second unit shot everyone impersonating panic while the cameras recorded the set burning down.

But the real pyrotechnics surrounding the making of *The Emperor of Aspiration* were unrelated to the razing of

Moreau's domain. By bringing the screenplay to syndicated columnist Louella Parsons and bemoaning the project's exalted status among certain Hollywood potentates, the Rowens ignited a firestorm that Miss Parsons and her arch-rival, Hedda Hopper, fueled almost daily. Sonya would not soon forget perusing the *Los Angeles Examiner* for August 14, 1941, and coming upon Miss Parsons's opening salvo.

Last week we enjoyed a visit from Nigel and Desmond Rowen, who make wholesome albeit not always profitable movies through Epiphany Studios.

The Rowan brothers lent me a script they'd acquired for an impending musical, The Emperor of Aspiration, *adapted by horror film has-been Sonya Orlova from a disgusting novel by the libertine writer H.G. Wells. This folly recently wrapped on the MGM lot under the aegis of Klaus Lamprecht.*

Among her many lapses in judgment, Miss Orlova has taken Wells's most blasphemous scene and press-ganged it into the cult of Charles Darwin. To appease their malicious creator, a chanting tribe of "Beast People" pledges "not to confuse natural selection with divine intervention" and "not to call ourselves the apex of creation" and so on, each time adding the Darwinian refrain, "Are we not animals?"

Perhaps Louis B. Mayer believes that, because Hedda Hopper has endorsed this travesty, he can release it with impunity. But having Miss Hopper tout a perverse motion picture is like having Mussolini recommend a bottle of poisoned Chianti. What else did you expect?

—

Upon reading Miss Parsons's egregious column, Miss Hopper consulted Sonya and Isaac about the blasphemous chant. They hastened to inform the bewildered columnist that Hollywood writers routinely put outrageous material in their screenplays for the fun of it, knowing it would be excised before the cameras rolled. Armed with this inside dope, Miss Hopper sat down at her typewriter and pounded out her riposte to Miss Parsons.

—

It amazes me that, after reporting on Hollywood happenings for the last thirty years or so, the fearsomely uninformed Louella Parsons still has no idea how motion pictures are actually made.

I refer to her recent attack on the new MGM musical The Emperor of Aspiration, *scheduled to open at Graustack's Oriental Movie Palace on December 10th. Although an early draft included a chorus of "Fur Folk" reveling in their connection to the natural world, scenarist Sonya Orlova and executive producer Isaac Bachman assure me they will omit the scene, having realized there's nothing to be gained from annoying moviegoers who share Miss Parsons's horror of biology.*

How amusing that my colleague would compare me to Benito Mussolini. If I am Il Duce, then Miss Parsons is Joseph Goebbels, propaganda minister for a paperhanger whose name often appears in the headlines these days. We can thank our lucky stars that free speech in our republic bows only to judicial interpretations of the First Amendment and not to the whims of autocrats like Herr Goebbels or tittle-tattlers like Miss Parsons.

—

While the post-production team worked around the clock to ready *The Emperor of Aspiration* for its world premiere, the inferno raged, with all sides getting burned. Miss Parsons approvingly quoted a Rowen brothers press release calling on "religious Americans" to stop patronizing films signed by Louis B. Mayer, "since MGM now stands for Morally Grotesque Movies." For several weeks running, Sonya was distressed to learn, the boycott made an appreciable dent in Leo the Lion's box-office receipts.

Rather less successful was the Rowens' plea for "all enemies of indecency" to travel to Culver City and picket the studio. On any given day, the protestors never numbered more than a dozen. Some picketers, when interviewed, blithely repeated rumors that *The Emperor of Aspiration* included scenes adapted from James Joyce's *Ulysses* and animated cartoon sequences based on Egon Schiele's pornographic drawings.

Thus it happened that the movie became a *cause célèbre* before anybody had actually seen it. Not a day went by without a pundit blustering about the necessity of reverence or the imperative of free speech. Walt Kelly, a young artist working for the Disney organization, provided the best such jibe, a three-panel strip showing the Rowens removing the blindfold from Lady Justice and using it to gag her.

For Nigel and Desmond, the camel's spine snapped—or so Sonya realized in retrospect—when Hedda Hopper interviewed Osmond Fraenkel, an attorney for the American Civil Liberties Union, on her newly launched radio program.

"We just learned that two textbook authors and God-botherers called Nigel and Desmond Rowen plan to destroy all existing prints of the Ape Woman movies," said Mr. Fraenkel, "an act our organization regards as tantamount to book burning. Let me entreat every curriculum materials commissioner in the nation to stop subsidizing the Jubilee Publishing Company."

Instead of waiting to see if Fraenkel's plea would affect sales of *Exploring Creation through Biology*, the Rowen brothers sent Sonya a threatening telegram, which she immediately shared with Isaac and Mr. Darwin.

THIS DONNYBROOK HAS GONE ON LONG ENOUGH STOP YOU BACHMAN & DR ORLOV MUST COME TO LOS FELIZ AT 8:00 TOMORROW NIGHT **STOP** WE HAVE DRAFTED SURRENDER TERMS!

"Who do they think is surrendering?" said Isaac.

"Pinnacle Pictures, I imagine," said Sonya.

"In a pig's eye."

"I'm coming, too," said Mr. Darwin.

"Good idea," said Isaac, who'd recently learned not only that Ungagi the Great's skull contained a transplanted human brain but also that his larynx had been reconfigured for speech.

"I won't turn those nincompoops upside down this time, but I'll unnerve them all the same," said Mr. Darwin.

"I don't know what you're talking about, Ungagi," said Isaac, "but I wish I'd been there."

As Sonya and Isaac mounted the portico of the Ennis House, Jordan the butler, wearing his distinctive grey morning coat, opened the door before she could ring the bell. His punctuality didn't surprise her, since the Rowens were expecting the Pinnacle contingent, though Vasily was evidently the most expected: the hall table held a bottle of vodka, a bottle of vermouth, and a martini glass.

"I hope we've not seen the last of the Ape Woman," said Jordan, beaming at Sonya.

"No new Korgora pictures on the horizon." She was pleased that, despite his employers' wishes, Jordan had become a fan. "But you might enjoy my mad scientist in *The Emperor of Aspiration*."

While Vasily swizzled up a martini, Jordan fixed on Mr. Darwin and asked, "That was you playing Dr. Pongowana, am I right, sir? Your stage name is Ungagi the Great?"

"Yes, but don't let it get around that I'm more or less a person. The fans want somebody who's a hundred percent gorilla."

"You can talk!" exclaimed Jordan.

"Upgraded voice box."

"The boys are watching *The Sign of the Cross*," said Jordan, leading the party through the maze of corridors. "They're planning a Technicolor remake."

They entered the parlor, where the movie screen displayed a long shot of Poppaea, wife of the Emperor Nero, bathing in asses' milk.

"Your guests have arrived," Jordan announced as Claudette Colbert blithely ordered her handmaidens around.

"Usher them to their seats," Nigel called from out of the darkness.

Jordan directed Sonya and her two human companions onto a sofa. Mr. Darwin eased his bulk into a mammoth leather chair.

"I saw this movie when it came out." Sonya pitched her voice toward the brothers' presumed location. "You'll have trouble topping it."

"Jordan, Dr. Orlov would like a vodka martini," said Desmond.

"We already took care of that," said Vasily, sipping.

"Might I suggest you turn off the projector?" said Isaac.

"Wilson Barrett wrote a pious play, but lots of Christian moviegoers detested DeMille's adaptation," said Nigel. "We're trying to figure out why, so we don't make the same mistakes."

"I suspect it had something to do with Poppaea going skinny dipping," said Sonya. "Let me suggest you also leave out the courtesan trying to seduce the heroine with her Dance of the Naked Moon."

"I smell a gorilla," said Desmond. "Brother Zolgar, you weren't invited."

"Then I guess I'll retire to the conservatory and eat the Persian rug," said Mr. Darwin.

"Ah, the beast *speaks*—or is that Al Jolson dubbing in your voice?" said Desmond.

"We came here to negotiate," said Isaac, "not to try spotting Claudette Colbert's nipples."

"Our terms are simple," said Nigel. "Epiphany Studios will compensate Dr. Orlov for his investment in *The Emperor of Aspiration*, and Mr. Bachman will instruct Mr. Mayer to bury the picture."

"My Aunt Fanny," said Isaac.

"Nobody instructs Mr. Mayer to do much of anything," noted Sonya.

"We're prepared to drop an additional five hundred thousand on top of the sum Dr. Orlov has already wasted on your fiasco," said Nigel.

"Fuck you," said Isaac.

"That is not a counteroffer," said Nigel.

"Or maybe it is," said Vasily.

"We don't have a counteroffer," said Isaac.

"The evening is young. You'll come up with something."

For the next ninety minutes, the Pinnacle contingent sat in the dark, brooding and fuming while Cecil B. DeMille filled the screen with Roman archers slaughtering Christians who'd assembled illegally; Joyzelle Joyner slithering up and down Elissa Landi in a blatantly lesbian gambit; and Nero's henchmen imprisoning scores of martyrs beneath the Colosseum prior to feeding them to lions and alligators—the whole pre-Code extravaganza intercut with Charles Laughton hamming it up in a toga, as if practicing for his not dissimilar role in *The Island of Lost Souls*.

"Okay, here are my terms," said Isaac. "*The Emperor of Aspiration* will start playing at Graustack's Oriental on December tenth as scheduled. Then, after your DeMille remake opens, instead of asking you for free passes, I'll buy tickets for all the top Pinnacle brass and their families."

"Just so you'll know—not everyone who attends the premiere of your dumb musical will be rooting for it," said Nigel with nuanced menace. "Half the membership of CAVE will be there, and so will—"

"CAVE?" said Sonya.

"The Coalition Against Vulgar Entertainment. We're also expecting large turnouts from the Catholic Legion of Decency and the Soldiers of Jehovah."

Large turnouts—the prediction was music to Sonya's ears. By all means, let's have phalanxes of philistines at the premiere. Bring on the CAVE men. Let the whole world see that the Rowens and their allies know even less about art than they do about biology.

"I'm told the ACLU plans to show up too," said Isaac.

"This sounds like a recipe for disaster," said Vasily. "Black eyes, split lips, concussions. I'm bringing my medical bag."

"Remove the vodka bottles, and you'll have more room for bandages," said Nigel.

The screen displayed a Roman arena. Dressed only in

garlands, a female martyr struggled against the thongs binding her to an upright wooden stake. A gorilla approached and eyed the woman with degenerate intentions.

"Please keep me in mind for that part," said Mr. Darwin, who'd evidently learned a thing or two about sarcasm during his years in Hollywood.

"Consider this, Isaac—it's not too late to cancel the premiere," said Desmond. "Such a huge protest will scandalize Mayer. He'll see to it you never make another movie."

"You can take your vulgarity coalition and shove it up your ass," said Isaac.

"Always a pleasure doing business with you, Isaac," said Nigel. "See you at the premiere. The popcorn's on me."

CHAPTER 5
HER FAVORITE APE

After gasping and groaning her way through a private screening in the MGM projection room, Sonya seriously considered skipping the world premiere. Apart from some agreeable Kalmar and Ruby songs and the lush fecundity of the artificial jungle, everything about *The Emperor of Aspiration* made her wince. She hated her performance as Moreau, hated the way Billie Burke had dubbed her song, hated how the Fur Folk seemed to have wandered in from a children's movie nobody in his right mind would take a child to see.

"In a week from Saturday I'm going to develop a splitting headache," she told Isaac that afternoon, "and I'll have to forgo the premiere."

"Most of the cast will be there, even some Fur Folk," he protested. "H.V. Kaltenborn's planning a live remote broadcast. He wants to call you, me, and your brother up to the NBC mike. The whole *world* will be waiting to hear from you."

As things shook out, history upstaged the opening of *Emperor of Aspiration* with an event of far greater gravity. Unlike Isaac's arguments, the surprise attack on the US naval fleet anchored at Pearl Harbor convinced Sonya to attend the premiere. When Kaltenborn invited her to address the radio audience, she would insist that Pinnacle Pictures was a patriotic studio where defeating the Empire of Japan mattered far more than box-office receipts.

The Pinnacle contingent arrived on the scene two hours ahead of the 8:00 p.m. showtime, Isaac having decided to reconnoiter the deployments of protestors and counter-protestors. Klaus Lamprecht had taken to bed with the flu, and Homer was in New York trying to talk CBS into renewing *Ticket to Tomorrow*, but everyone else had gathered, as arranged, on the sidewalk outside the Suncoast Hotel, across the street from Graustack's Oriental Movie Palace. Sonya and Celeste wore white satin evening gowns. Isaac had dusted off his tuxedo. Vasily, thus far sober, had opted for a preposterous pink three-piece suit, and he'd indeed brought along his medical bag. Mr. Darwin, twirling a walking stick, looked dapper in his black cape and top hat.

They rode the elevator to the hotel roof and crossed the terrace to a wrought-iron balustrade. Brilliant beacons swept the rose-colored clouds with crisscrossing shafts of light, as if Cecil B. DeMille were about to project his latest epic on a piece of sky he'd leased from God. At regular intervals the beams struck Graustack's Oriental, a magnificent mess of a building featuring a scaled-down pagoda and a Shinto temple gateway. Hollywood Boulevard thronged with movie fans, some surrounding an elevated platform supporting NBC's ad hoc radio studio, others engulfing a makeshift podium holding two Fox Movietone News cameras. The crowd's demeanor, restless and feverish, betrayed not only post-Pearl Harbor anxiety but also, Sonya sensed, a frantic desire to get their faces into the newsreel.

CAVE and its allies would obviously be staging a more

colorful protest than the ACLU. Barely fifty in number, Osmond Fraenkel's brigade milled around in boring blazers, ties, and fedoras, holding up anodyne placards declaring FREEDOM OF THOUGHT IS NEVER FOR NAUGHT and GOD BLESS THE FIRST AMENDMENT and SUPPORT THE SEPARATION OF CHURCH AND BIOLOGY. The opposition, nearly a thousand strong, included a faction dressed in gorilla costumes, their signs reading I'M NOT YOUR ANCESTOR and DETHRONE THE EMPEROR OF BLASPHEMY and DOWN WITH PROSTITUTION, PERVERSION, PORNOGRAPHY, AND PERMISSIVENESS. Costumed as the persecuted Christians in *The Sign of the Cross*, the other CAVE members waved 1,000-foot reels of 35mm film over their heads like Gypsies rattling tambourines.

After everybody descended to the parking garage, Isaac led them into the alley behind the hotel, where a stone-faced black man, who gave his name as Everett Blair, sat behind the wheel of a sleek white rental limousine. With consummate professionalism Mr. Blair drove the Pinnacle contingent through the multitudes lining Vine Street, then turned onto Hollywood Boulevard and joined the queue of limousines crawling between sawhorse barriers toward the theater. An instant later H.V. Kaltenborn's rapid-fire radio voice, amplified by a public-address system, announced the arrival of the first *Emperor of Aspiration* stars.

"Ladies and gentlemen, it's the beauteous Hedy Lamarr and the urbane Walter Pidgeon!"

The crowd whistled, hooted, and roared.

"I just spotted the red carpet," Mr. Blair reported.

"It's the stunning Lena Horne, the genial Mickey Rooney, and the hilarious Jimmy Durante, who play some of the Fur Folk you've heard so much about!"

Shouts and cheers resounded through the winter air.

The limousine lurched to a halt. A young man in an usher's brass-buttoned uniform opened the door and led Sonya to the forecourt of Graustack's Oriental. As she passed a pair of decorative marble Foo dogs, galaxies of flashbulbs exploded. Her retinas vibrated with the afterimages.

"Ashley Wilkes himself—the distinguished Leslie Howard—sharing the ride with the duke of derring-do, Errol Flynn, and the belle of buxom, Mae West!"

Sonya followed Isaac and Vasily up a plywood staircase toward the improvised radio studio. Stepping onto the rostrum, she glimpsed Mr. Howard, Mr. Flynn, and Miss West as they crossed a facsimile of an Asian footbridge and started along the red carpet. Movie fans leaned over the burgundy velvet ropes, waving autograph books like aquarium workers offering fish to dolphins, but the Hollywood royalty merely smiled and walked on.

"The world's favorite gorilla has joined the promenade," said Kaltenborn. "Ungagi the Great enchanted us in the Ape Woman series, and he plays a similar role in tonight's picture. Accompanying Ungagi is new-kid-on-the-block Celeste Torrance, cast as the hybrid M'ling." He shifted his gaze from the red carpet to the sawhorse lane. "Looks like the final limo has arrived and—hang onto your hats—it's the eternally captivating Jean Arthur and the perpetually suave Cary Grant!"

Sonya surveyed the hubbub below. As they strolled down the carpet, Celeste and Mr. Darwin paused to sign autograph books. God knew what these fans made of the gorilla's nearly human writing skills.

No sooner had they reached the theater entrance than some sort of commotion or anomaly caught Mr. Darwin's attention. He grabbed Celeste's hand and, brushing past Jean Arthur and Cary Grant, led her back down the carpet toward the NBC rostrum.

Kaltenborn, a balding man with a pince-nez and a negligible moustache, gestured Isaac over to the lectern with its bouquet of microphones. "Ladies and gentlemen, we're honored to have the executive producer of *The Emperor of Aspiration* with us tonight, plus Dr. Vasily Orlov, vice president of Pinnacle Pictures, and Miss Sonya Orlova, who wrote the script and appears as the villainous Dr. Moreau. Mr. Bachman, perhaps you'd like to address your thousands of well-wishers on Hollywood Boulevard and out there in radio land."

"Everyone at Pinnacle is grateful for the support the Hollywood community has shown *The Emperor of Aspiration*," Isaac blathered, "an entertainment we believe offers moviegoers not only food for thought but also dessert for delectation."

"It defames the Almighty!" screamed a gorilla-suited protestor.

"Dr. Orlov, have you anything to add to Mr. Bachman's remarks?" asked Kaltenborn.

"Only that God is probably the sort of Supreme Being who can look after His own reputation," said Vasily.

Suddenly Mr. Darwin appeared on the rostrum, Celeste in tow. He drew Sonya aside and whispered, "The Rowens are here, and they've brought a *fire* with them."

"Huh?"

"Miss Orlova, would you care to say a few words?" asked Kaltenborn.

"A man is not a monkey!" screamed a *Sign of the Cross* martyr with a frothy grey beard.

Sonya marched up to the lectern and began declaiming in her most solemn Golemoiselle voice. "As we all know, three days ago the conflict convulsing our world came to the shores of America, and Mr. Roosevelt tells us we are now at war. If you're here to celebrate our Technicolor picture, we ask that tomorrow you employ the same degree of enthusiasm in cheering our troops as they march against General Tojo. If you came to protest our star-studded musical, we ask you to consider redirecting your discontent toward defeating the Axis powers."

A squad of police officers attempted to close the limousine lane, but before they could set any barriers in place, a blue pickup truck stopped outside the theater. The load-bed held Nigel and Desmond Rowen plus an iron cauldron containing the fire that had distressed Mr. Darwin, the orange flames darting amid the floating embers like demon tongues snatching up locusts.

Now a parade of *Sign of the Cross* martyrs came marching toward the forecourt, holding their 35mm film reels aloft. Upon reaching the pickup truck, the lead martyr, a ruddy, well-favored man with silver hair, stretched his arm skyward and handed his reel to Nigel.

"*The Ape Woman Returns* teaches our children they're animals!" cried Nigel, pointing to the reel before tossing it into the flames.

As the nitrate stock caught fire, a volcanic explosion rattled the cauldron, followed by billows of black smoke. The aftershocks reverberated up and down the boulevard.

Undaunted, the next martyr in line, a handsome, middle-aged woman, surrendered her reel to Desmond.

"God made us in his own image, not King Kong's!" he cried. "Don't let *The Ape Woman Strikes Back* tell you otherwise!"

Desmond fed a thousand feet of film to the fire, triggering another eruption. The air grew pungent with incinerated celluloid.

Now Nigel received a reel from a third martyr, a gaunt man with a goiter, and hurled it into the cauldron. *"The Ape Woman Meets the Blood Demon* turns Genesis into gobbledygook!" he proclaimed as the explosion vaporized eleven minutes of Sonya's favorite Korgora entry.

"The Japs are coming *here* next!" wailed a blonde female martyr wearing a large silver cross. "Their carriers have been spotted off Catalina!"

"Graustack's Oriental is a fifth column!" added a rotund male martyr holding a shepherd's crook. "That pagoda is a radio tower for guiding Nip bombers to LA!"

"Ladies and gentlemen, I implore you!" cried Kaltenborn. "Ignore the fear-mongers among us!"

The mob surged across the forecourt like frenzied peasants in a Frankenstein picture. Goaded by the martyrs, the moviegoers began dismantling the façade of Graustack's Oriental. The pagoda crashed onto the concrete sidewalk like a felled redwood, scattering its lath, struts, and cornices everywhere. No broadcast equipment or Japanese radio operators emerged from the debris. Next the Shinto temple gate crumbled, its elegant timbers spilling onto the boulevard. The police waded into the crowd with drawn nightsticks, but their efforts to control the chaos merely compounded it.

"Folks, please!" wailed Kaltenborn.

The rioters went looking for other targets. They tore the footbridge to pieces, knocked over the Foo dogs, and leveled the box office with its decorative carving of a chubby Buddha. The Fox Movietone crew judiciously removed their cameras from the podium, which collapsed an instant later in a heap of lumber and bunting, even as the NBC rostrum listed to and fro like a trawler in a typhoon.

While Sonya hugged the lectern, Vasily and Celeste started down the trembling staircase, Mr. Darwin shambling after them. On reaching the penultimate riser, Vasily vaulted to the relative safety of the sidewalk. Celeste followed. Sonya released the lectern and rushed across the rostrum to the top of the staircase—just in time to see Mr. Darwin attempt the leap. Despite his great bulk he managed to become airborne, his top hat flying away, but then he collided with a freckled, carrot-topped police officer, and they both tumbled onto the sidewalk.

The officer scrambled to his feet. Still on his back, Mr. Darwin flailed about like a flipped turtle. Apparently the officer didn't recognize the gorilla as the highly domesticated Ungagi the Great, for he suddenly yanked out his pistol.

"He's harmless!" cried Sonya.

And then the unimaginable happened. Standing over Ungagi, the officer pointed his gun at the helpless ape's broad, sloping brow. He squeezed the trigger. Chips of Mr. Darwin's skull flew in all directions. Blood geysered forth.

Sonya screamed, and she continued screaming as the pillars supporting the rostrum gave way, hurtling her into space.

Descending, she braced herself for the impact. She did not expect fire, but that's what came next, the raging flames of the inferno wrought by the Rowens. An instant later, as if every god in the universe had turned against her, she plummeted into the cauldron and blacked out.

For an indeterminate interval—hours, days, weeks—who could say?—she floated on a lake blooming with carnivorous algae—or so it seemed—and stocked with stinging jellyfish. Her skull became a throbbing mass of fissured crystal. In time a low male voice broke against her consciousness like surf hitting a jetty.

"Sonya, can you hear me? Sonya? Sonya?"

It sounded like her brother, but she wasn't sure. "V-Vasily?"

"Lie still. You're in Pico Rivera—the recovery room."

Slowly she blinked. Vasily loomed over her, exhaling vodka fumes. She blinked again. Bright red veins entwined his eyes. She sensed she was on her back and in a bed.

"My h-head … hurts."

"I'm not surprised," said Vasily.

"What time is it?"

"Morning."

She lifted her hand, which gradually came into focus. A hand, yes, but not of the human sort, the digits being usually thick and the back hairy.

"I'm … not d-dead?"

"You're entirely alive," said Vasily, "but you've had a— that is, your *mind* has had a … transplant."

"A what?"

"Transplant. The body donor was Mr. Darwin."

"I'm a g-gorilla?"

"Nurse Torrance, help my sister to understand."

Dressed in her starched white uniform, Celeste glided into view.

"Hi there, Sonya."

"A gorilla? Please, not really…"

Having lodged in Mr. Darwin's brain, the bullet should have killed him, Celeste explained, but he was nevertheless alive when Vasily and the chauffeur placed him in the rental limo. Vasily had retrieved his medical bag from the back seat, and then Mr. Blair and Mr. Darwin had sped away, bound for the Orlov Clinic. A phone call from Celeste had alerted Nurse Cassidy to the patient's imminent arrival.

After the police had pulled Sonya's unconscious body from the fire, Vasily gave her a morphine injection and then, realizing she was minutes from death, arranged her transport by stretcher to a ground-floor function room in the Suncoast Hotel. Assisted by Celeste, he went to work with scalpel and jigsaw, performing what amounted to battlefield surgery. Taking care not to abrade the tissues or expose them to particulate matter, he and Celeste had packed Sonya's brain in ice chips from the hotel kitchen. The police took possession of the corpse, wrapping it in blankets and promising Vasily they would guard his sister's remains until this bizarre situation sorted itself out.

"How d-did my brain … g-get here?" asked Sonya.

"Taxi," said Celeste.

"Late last night, we all collected around Mr. Darwin in the surgical theater," said Yvonne Cassidy, appearing at

Sonya's bedside. "He couldn't speak, but he understood our words."

"We presented him with a difficult choice," said Celeste. "The X-ray revealed a bullet lodged so deep in his mesencephelon that we could save his life only by devoting three hours to removing his entire brain, extracting the slug, and repairing the damaged tissue."

"Knowing that, without a medulla regulating the heart and lungs, his noncerebral tissues would die in the interim," said Yvonne. "To keep the invaluable Charles Darwin on the planet, we would have to freeze his brain in hopes of eventually locating a body donor."

"The second option would find us removing Mr. Darwin's cortical hemispheres," said Celeste, "and spending three hours transplanting Sonya Orlova's disembodied brain into the decerebrated but otherwise healthy gorilla."

"Knowing that, because of the slug, irreversible necrosis would destroy Mr. Darwin's neurons even if we froze them," said Yvonne.

"A d-difficult choice, y-yes," said Sonya.

"Mr. Darwin made a victory sign," said Celeste. "Two fingers. The second option."

"So he s-sacrificed himself for me?" said Sonya.

"Correct," said Celeste.

"Without hesitation," said Yvonne.

Sonya began to weep, Vasily having evidently successfully conjoined her conscious mind to her affective nervous system. "My d-dear Mr. Darwin, *tu as fait un b-beau geste.*"

"Yes, that's what it was," said Yvonne. "A beautiful

gesture. He has nearly breathed his last, but the necrosis hasn't yet reached his speech centers. There's still time to say goodbye."

"Can you walk thirty paces to my consulting room?" asked Vasily.

"*Le plus beau des gestes,*" said Sonya, blotting her tears with the back of her hairy hand.

Assisted by her companions, she hoisted her simian bulk free of the bed. Moving on knuckles and toes, she crept out of the recovery room and down the hallway. Her head throbbed. Her joints felt stiff. The oscillations of her male member unnerved her. As she entered the consulting room, her vision sharpened noticeably, but the Chagall reproductions on the walls lacked vibrancy. The carpet smelled of mildew.

Bathed in a translucent broth of nutrients, Mr. Darwin's detached and dying brain occupied a ten-gallon aquarium resting on a white-sheeted gurney. The cortical tissues, coral in color, pulsed like a blowfish inflating and deflating. A dozen electrified probes jutted from each hemisphere, their wires snaking out of the aquarium and splitting into two clusters, one set connected to a microphone on a floor stand, the other to a radio console on Vasily's desk. Rising from the console like an outsized daffodil, a cone-shaped Victrola speaker filled the room with a soft gurgling evidently generated by the scientist's cerebral impulses.

Cautiously Sonya approached the microphone. "Mr. Darwin?"

The brainwave gurgling increased in volume. A male voice, laden with static, crackled out of the speaker. "*Call me ... Charles.*"

She surveyed the throbbing hemispheres. "Oh, my dear Mr. Darwin—Charles—how can I ever repay you?"

The gurgling grew louder yet. Tiny gas particles swarmed through the broth like champagne bubbles. "*If somebody said that in ... a Korgora script ... Homer would make you ... rewrite.*"

She squeezed her brother's wrist. "Isn't there anything ...?"

"*There's nothing for it,*" said the brain before Vasily could answer. "*Dear Sonya, I can no longer ... be with you.*"

"I owe you so much." Reaching past the microphone, she caressed the front of the aquarium. "We all do. You brought us home."

"*And now the time has come ... for me to cede my place ... to another primate. 'Death is the tool that shapes.'*"

The tissues lost their salmon hue and began turning gray.

"*Ave atque vale,*" said Vasily.

"It was a privilege caring for you," said Yvonne.

"I hope there's a heaven," said Celeste.

"Goodbye, dear friend," said Sonya.

"'*Loss is the scythe that—*'"

And then the gurgling stopped.

Now that the Second World War had come to occupy, day and night, the collective American imagination, nobody worried much about whether the nation's youth were receiving an adequate education in biology. But Sonya and her colleagues could still claim *The Emperor of Aspiration* had accomplished its purpose, for almost everyone who saw the Fox Movietone newsreel of the premiere had decided the Rowens were dangerous loons. Before long, thousands of parents were demanding that, whatever biology textbook their sons and daughters were reading, whether it exalted, attacked, or ignored Charles Darwin, it must not bear the Jubilee trademark.

After the company went out of business, the brothers poured their energies into their Technicolor remake of *The Sign of the Cross*, staying solvent by producing a beloved series of two-reel comedies featuring the Four Goofballs, Binx, Bollix, Boink, and Yo-Yo. When it came to replacing the Rowens' *Exploring Creation through Biology*, textbook commissioners settled for whatever prewar product was reasonably priced and easily obtained. George Hunter's post-Scopes, Darwin-free *New Civic Biology* was the most common substitute. Truman Moon's God-friendly *Biology for Beginners* also enjoyed an uptick in sales.

As for *The Emperor of Aspiration*, film critics of all persuasions agreed it was the most ill-conceived and ludicrous motion picture of 1941. Today, of course, this baroque adaptation of H.G. Wells is beloved by connoisseurs of unintentional camp, and it also enjoys a following among gourmands of guilty pleasures. Contemporary moviegoers, however, discouraged by the reviews and deterred by word-of-mouth, found other things to do with their time.

"Like the hybrids Dr. Moreau creates in her laboratory, *The Emperor of Aspiration* is a cobbled-together monstrosity," said *Daily Variety*.

"An overcooked plum pudding that fails to provide even one spoonful of Christmas cheer," warned the *Boston Globe*. "The climax is full of *Sturm und Drang* that provides only squirms and pangs."

"Lamprecht and company seem to think they're making an acerbic point about the tyranny religion can exert over the human mind," complained the *Chicago Tribune*. "But these days, surely, a more worthy target would be secular dictators like *Der Führer* and *Il Duce*."

"Who, exactly, do the makers of *The Emperor of Aspiration* imagine will patronize this confused and tedious circus?" asked the *New York Times*.

—

Perhaps they're anticipating scads of school children. Yes, youngsters will probably enjoy the Fur Folk, but what will they make of Dr. Moreau's salacious plans to breed her souped-up panther with a couple of shipwrecked grifters?

Maybe the producers expect adult aficionados of political satire to show up, which would explain the mordant characterization of Moreau as a demagogue, but then why subject these same urbane moviegoers to Jimmy Durante playing a Rhinoceros Man?

Sometimes the film seems slanted toward armchair philosophers, hence the high-flying speeches about the web of life, but, if so, why did Sonya Orlova litter her script with sentimental laments from people who wish they'd been born animals?

—

"I'm told that, because of the huge budget," said Isaac, "our movie is on its way to becoming the biggest flop ever released by Metro."

"So much for my shrewd investment," said Vasily. "Thank God black-market brain surgery still pays well."

"I wish Mr. Darwin had lived to see the collapse of Jubilee," said Homer.

"I miss him so much," said Celeste.

Sonya, weeping outsized ape tears, said nothing.

As the global cataclysm dragged on, Sonya fought a war of her own against grief, regret, and the occasional urge to throw herself off the highest balcony of Medusa Manor. Living inside the very flesh and bones once occupied by Mr. Darwin prompted her to mourn him all the more, and yet, according to Vasily, there was no point in trying to find a second body donor for her—not on death row, not in a cancer ward, not anywhere. The necessarily hasty transfer of her cortical hemispheres to Zolgar's body had so thoroughly fused the connection between Sonya's brain and the gorilla's spinal cord that further relocations were out of the question.

At first it seemed that her new physiognomy would take a toll on her love life. But then, over the course of several surgeries, Vasily managed to modify her ostensible gender and restore her customary passions. In time their novel situation became for Sonya and Homer a source of genuine carnal satisfaction. It spoke well of him, she thought, that he was prepared to explore a zone that lay so far beyond the bounds of conventional erotic practices. When she praised his adventuresome spirit, Homer breezily replied, paraphrasing Terence's maxim. "As a science-fiction writer, I say that nothing alien is alien to me."

In the spring of 1945, the Allies rang down the curtain on the European Theater, and that summer the war in the Pacific ended following the atomic attacks on Hiroshima and Nagasaki. With peace on earth came a renewed sense of purpose for Sonya. Her career as the Woman of a Thousand Faces was over, of course, and the whole world knew it, for the Fox Movietone News crew had caught her accidental incineration on 35mm film. The trained ape Ungagi the Great was also obviously unavailable for motion-picture roles, a Movietone camera having recorded him being shot in the head at point-blank range. And so the ever resourceful Sonya simply reinvented herself as Janga of the Jungle, the whimsical persona of a fictional expatriate, Nadiya Petrova, newly arrived in the United States from Ukraine.

As the decade wound down, Isaac Bachman, who'd gone to work for Sam Katzman at Monogram, helped Miss Petrova win roles in Tarzan adventures, Charlie Chan mysteries, circus pictures, and horror comedies. So compelling was Sonya in her Janga parts that film crews didn't question her quirky refusal to remove her gorilla suit between takes. Isaac, meanwhile, satisfied that his favorite actress had achieved a viable new identity, retired from the movie business, moved north, and spent his remaining years operating a winery in the Napa Valley. His prize-winning vintage was a blood-red cabernet called Nocturnia.

THAT TROUBLES OUR MONKEY AGAIN.

Female descendant of Marine Ascidian:—"REALLY, MR. DARWIN, SAY WHAT YOU LIKE ABOUT MAN; BUT I WISH YOU WOULD LEAVE MY EMOTIONS ALONE!"

"I'm here today with Ukrainian movie star Nadiya Petrova," said Hedda Hopper, kicking off the latest installment of her radio show. "Though I must tell my listeners I still don't know what Miss Petrova looks like, because of course she's wearing her Janga suit."

"Oh, it's much more than a *suit*," said Sonya in a sweetly scolding tone. "Janga is who I *am*. Nadiya Petrova is just the person who signs the contracts and cashes the checks."

"Such a charming affectation, and I'm sure there's a beautiful woman under all that fur. I thought you were captivating opposite Johnny Weissmuller in *Tarzan's Final Challenge*. You were also a treat in that Saturday matinee serial, *Rocket to the Hidden Kingdom*. What's next for Nadiya Petrova?"

"I'm scheduled to play the title character's devoted gorilla companion in a John Carradine vehicle called *Horror of Rasputin*."

"Nadiya, be a dear. Remove your ape head, so I can describe your lovely face to all the people out there in radio land."

"Hedda, I could no more do that than Harpo could come on your show and recite Shakespearean sonnets."

Despite her appearance on *Hedda Hopper's Hollywood* and similar programs, Sonya's hoax was not primarily about giving herself a second career in the movies. Her real objective was to continue the worthy educational project—common ancestors! reproductive fitness! the tree of life!—she'd begun with Mr. Darwin back in 1936. If she could find a Korgora print that had somehow survived the

Rowens' purge, then Janga could start giving guest talks in high-school biology classes, beguiling the students with her simian charisma while highlighting the exciting scientific ideas woven into the franchise's absurd premise.

Late in the summer of 1951, Sonya tracked down a contraband, third-generation, 16mm dupe of *The Ape Woman Returns*. Using a Moviola viewer, a pair of rewinds, and a hot splicer, she condensed it from sixty-eight minutes to forty, so it would fit into a single class period, and of course she left intact Dr. Rangorst's explanation of natural selection (keyed to the freakish reptiles he'd fashioned through controlled breeding). Much her delight, she learned that scores of science teachers, fed up with the *de facto* extraction of Darwin from the biology curriculum, were eager to have Janga as a guest lecturer. At some point during her presentation, a teenage smart-ass would invariably ask her to remove her gorilla head, and she would reply, "The Lone Ranger never takes off his mask."

Each talk ended with Sonya rhapsodizing about the loom of life and the great tapestry that was its issue, unfurling everywhere in space and time. Through her acting ability alone she made the pupils (some of them, anyway) see the woven wonder in their minds, this fabric that enfolded every bird, beast, and blossom that now lived and had ever lived and would ever live, each thread begetting the next, so that by following the filaments you could, if so inclined, link a macaque to a mollusk, a tortoise to a tulip, a bear to a bush, or a prophet to a paramecium.

"Charles Darwin gave us citizenship papers," she told the teenagers. "The Earth is our home."

Although these weren't precisely the best years of her life—nothing could top her reign as Hollywood's horror queen—she greatly enjoyed herself on the Janga circuit. The LA Coroner's Office had, of course, declared her dead, an indisputable verdict given the Fox Movietone footage of her fall into the cauldron. Nevertheless, with Vasily's assistance she drafted an *ex post facto* will bequeathing her earthly possessions to her siblings, who immediately gave them back, so that she retained her mansion, automobile, bank account, and wardrobe (though only the hats and the cloaks still fit). Meanwhile, she and Homer continued cultivating the joys of cross-species affection, and because Zolgar was evidently just out of adolescence when the Rowens abducted him, she expected that her borrowed body would remain healthy for at least another forty years.

On October 4, 1957, the Russians launched Sputnik, the first artificial orbiting satellite, sparking fear among America's leaders that, when it came to science and mathematics, the US public schools had fallen behind their Soviet counterparts. Eleven months later, Congress passed the National Defense Education Act, underwriting the development of rigorous teaching and learning resources. The adoption of Darwin-oriented biology textbooks happened piecemeal, of course, with some state commissions assenting only to curriculum materials that replaced "evolution" with euphemisms such as "growth" and "development," but by 1967—the year that the Butler Act, wellspring of the Scopes Trial, was overturned by the Tennessee legislature—Sonya felt confident that she and Mr. Darwin were winning their very good fight.

Of all the classroom visits Sonya made as Janga of the Jungle, the most remarkable found her back in familiar Southern California surroundings. On June 17, 1956 (a full sixteen months before America's Sputnik trauma), she brought her abridged *Return of the Ape Woman* print to Inglewood Senior High School. Her sponsor was Carmen Salazar, an exuberant biology teacher who had even the bullies and greasers wrapped around her little finger.

After the presentation, Mrs. Salazar invited Sonya to dinner at her house, adding, mysteriously, "There's something I want to show you."

"I would love to come," said Sonya, "but, you see, well…"

"Yes?"

"It's like this, Mrs. Salazar. I'm not really Nadiya Petrova in a gorilla suit. I couldn't take off this fur if I wanted to."

"I know. You're the Woman of a Thousand Faces."

"How in the world …?"

"I hope you will accept my invitation, Miss Orlova, even though we're having leftovers tonight."

Thus did Sonya find herself seated at the dining-room table in a tiled-roof ranch house in Morningside Park. While Carmen tossed the beans-and-greens salad, her husband did the cooking—or, rather, the reheating: crab cakes and fish sticks. Like his wife, Rafael was a teacher, instructing young minds in physics and astronomy at

Maywood Senior High. The Salazars' twin sons, eighth graders Luis and Abel, laid out the place settings. Their daughter, Ofelia, soon to enter first grade, said the grace.

"Miss Orlova, have you any idea how hard it is these days to find a textbook publisher willing to assert that the earth goes around the sun?" said Rafael with mock distress.

"The censoring of heliocentrism is a scandal," the gorilla-woman replied, deadpan, as she piled her plate high with salad. "Call me Sonya."

The children alternately ate their seafood and stared wide-eyed at their parents' hairy guest, whom Carmen had introduced as "a genuine Congo gorilla who came to America to get a better brain."

"I should've realized you don't eat fish," said Rafael apologetically, gesturing toward Sonya's plate.

"Once upon a time I did."

"You don't *smell* like a gorilla," said Ofelia.

"I take baths, just like you."

"So there I was," said Carmen, "watching *The Ape Woman Returns* with the class, casually noting that we're hearing Sonya Orlova's distinctive voice not only from Pongowana but also from Korgora—and suddenly it dawns on me: the vocal inflections and speech cadences of our special guest, Miss Petrova, are the same ones coming from the gorilla and her alter ego on the screen! Today's classroom visitor was the movie star I'd loved as a teenager in all those Countess Nocturnia and Golemoiselle movies!"

"You have a good ear," said Sonya.

"So I decided that during the *Aspiration* premiere some skilled physician must have—"

"My brother is LA's foremost unlicensed neurosurgeon," said Sonya.

"Your *brother*?"

"Dr. Vasily Orlov."

"He must've removed the brain of the dying Miss Orlova and transplanted it into Ungagi the Great."

"That's *impossible*," said Rafael. "It's like something out of a mad-scientist melodrama."

"Truth is stranger than horror movies," said Sonya.

"So there's no such person as Nadiya Petrova?" asked Rafael, and Sonya nodded.

"I'm confused about one thing," said Carmen. "Ungagi was a male gorilla, whereas you seem to be—"

"It's called sexual reassignment surgery," said Sonya.

"I see," said Carmen.

"My head is exploding," said Rafael.

"Dad," said Luis, "can Abel and I watch *Alfred Hitchcock Presents* tonight if we don't ask you to explain sexual reassignment surgery?"

"*Hitchcock Presents*?" said Rafael, scowling. "No, it will give you nightmares."

"Whereas spending an evening with a sexually reassigned gorilla whose skull contains a transplanted human brain will set sugarplums dancing in their heads," said Carmen.

"I think Mom just talked Dad into it," said Abel to Luis.

"Can Miss Orlova come *tomorrow* night, too?" asked Ofelia.

All during dessert, the twins chattered excitedly about the upcoming *Hitchcock Presents* offering, listed as "The Creeper" in the *Los Angeles Examiner*. The title brought a lump to Sonya's throat. Her late friend and colleague Rondo Hatton had memorably portrayed a madman called the Creeper in two sturdy little grade-B efforts, *House of Horrors* and *The Brute Man*, and he was equally effective playing heavies in *The Pearl of Death*, *The Spider Woman Strikes Back*, and *Jungle Captive*. Poor old acromegalic Rondo, who, owing to his grotesque features, symptoms of a defective pituitary gland, never needed make-up to play a monster.

While the twins washed the dishes, alternately grousing about the chore and giggling at each other's knock-knock jokes, Carmen escorted Sonya to her sewing room. Fluorescent lights flooded the space with a homogenous glow, revealing an elaborate miniature exhibit resting on a plywood platform. The dioramas celebrated three of Sonya's hits from the early 1930s—*Evil of Nocturnia*, *Cry of the She-Wolf*, and *Tomb of Golemoiselle*—and each featured not only a eight-inch-high ceramic monster but also an important secondary character: vampire hunter, werewolf expert, insane rabbi.

"These are amazing," said Sonya. "Did you make them?"

"Everybody needs a hobby."

Carmen drew her attention to a second set of dioramas

ranging across the adjacent worktable. The display included Dr. Rangorst's underground lair from *The Ape Woman Returns*, the insane asylum from *Spawn of the Ape Woman*, and the Transylvania castle from *The Ape Woman Meets the Blood Demon*.

"Believe it or not, the first Korgora film convinced me to study the life sciences," said Carmen. "I'd never heard of extinct common ancestors before."

"Could you please say that again? You'd never heard of—"

"Extinct common ancestors."

"And that's why you became—"

"A biology teacher."

A figurine in the corner of the *Ape Woman Returns* diorama caught Sonya's eye. Standing behind the ceramic Dr. Rangorst was a tall character wearing a broad-brimmed hat plus a dark cloak draped over his shoulders.

"Who might that be—God?" asked Sonya.

"Look closer."

Sonya plucked the figurine from Rangorst's lair and studied the bulbous nose, untrimmed beard, tired eyes, and soft smile—familiar features, for over the years she'd contemplated many photographs of the celebrated scientist.

"It's a terrific likeness."

"He was present in spirit when Rangorst explained the analogy between natural selection and controlled breeding, so I added him to the scene."

"I knew him," said Sonya.

"I feel as if I knew him, too."

"No, I mean I *really* knew him."
"Of course. Would you like to have it?"
"You mean it's a gift?"
"Thank you for visiting my class today."
"I loved him so much."

The grounds of Medusa Manor included a half-acre especially dear to Sonya's heart, the south terrace, where a gentle knoll sustained a eucalyptus tree, its foliage shading a marble birdbath rising from the hill like a baptismal font. A wrought-iron bench gave her a front-row seat at the daily ablutions of sparrows, tanagers, finches, magpies, and—on rare occasions—hummingbirds.

Two days after her dinner with the Salazars, Sonya carefully wedged her Charles Darwin figurine into the crook of the tree. There it remained: day in, day out—year in, year out. From this vantage the miniature scientist could observe not only avian species visiting the birdbath but also bumblebees negotiating the clover, beetles colonizing the rose bushes, and bougainvillea enswathing the sundial.

The years coalesced into decades, and the ceramic Mr. Darwin continued surveying the scene. Late in 1977, Homer retired from his job as the producer of ABC's science-fiction television series, *Via Galactica*, sold his houseboat, and moved in with Sonya. The subsequent spring began on a heartening note, with Celeste Torrance receiving an Oscar nomination as Best Supporting Actress for her performance as aviation pioneer Ruth Nichols in the Amelia Earhart biopic, *The Other Side of the Sky*. But then came a dreadful autumn, which found Vasily hospitalized for liver disease. He died on Pearl Harbor Day.

Before the year was out, the Rowens finally realized what a generally terrible person their grandfather had been, a man who'd driven his own son to suicide and thought nothing of crediting himself with other scientists' discoveries. Eventually they forsook their Genesis-inflected understanding of the universe and started an ashram in Santa Barbara.

Late in the afternoon on her eighty-second birthday, Sonya sat before her birdbath, savoring a glass of Chablis while watching her favorite sort of songbird, an orange-headed Western tanager, fluttering its parasites away. Mr. Darwin had once remarked that the bird family, so varied, so beautiful, so paradoxical (many species were flightless), was perhaps "the most elegant bell-tower on the evolutionary cathedral that biologists are steadily building." Indeed, a recent *Scientific American* article made a case against regarding dinosaurs as a closed chapter in the chronicles of life on earth, for many species had almost certainly evolved into birds. Sonya could practically hear her Darwin figurine thinking through the problem.

But of course! Dinosaurs laid eggs—just like birds. Many evidently had feathers. They were arguably warm-blooded. And how to describe the archaeopteryx if not as a small-toothed, bony-tailed coelurosaur that—with its plumage, wings, and hollow bones—was well on its way to becoming something else?

An immense crow glided out of the cloudless sky,

crying harshly, bound for the eucalyptus. A female, Sonya decided. Reaching her destination, the imposing creature, black as Nocturnia's cape, seized Mr. Darwin with her clawed feet and pulled him free of the crook. Startled, the tanager shot away. Still cawing, flapping furiously, the crow soared into the heavens bearing the figurine and vanished.

The tanager flew back to the birdbath. Sonya sipped Chablis. When she described the scene to Homer that night, would she dare tell him what she thought was really going on?

Yes, she would.

"Aren't you being anthropomorphic?" he responded.

"I suppose so. And yet I believe the crow knew exactly what particular person she was spiriting away."

"Does she plan to use Mr. Darwin as a prop while lecturing her fellow crows?" asked Homer. "Will she teach the flock about common ancestors and reproductive fitness?"

"It's possible."

He offered her a tilted smile. "I see."

"And after the crow is finished with the figurine, dear Homer, she'll return it to the eucalyptus. This won't happen right away, of course, not tomorrow or the next day or even the day after. But in time Mr. Darwin will come back to Medusa Manor, and he'll find you and me sitting on the south terrace, and we'll toast him with our wine, and he'll tell us all about life among the dinosaurs."

ACKNOWLEDGMENTS

Throughout the writing—and rewriting—of *Behold the Ape*, I drew upon a smorgasbord of sources. Early in the composition process, my son Christopher Morrow enlightened and inspired me with his knowledge of evolutionary biology while we toured the dinosaur exhibits in the American Museum of Natural History. As the manuscript took root and grew, I incorporated many facts supplied by my two favorite connoisseurs of Hollywood lore: Joe Kaufman, my man on the ground in LA, and Joe Adamson, old friend and film historian extraordinaire. In his letter accepting the manuscript for publication by WordFire Press, Kevin J. Anderson astutely diagnosed two problems I was grateful to learn about and gratified to—I hope—solve.

I must also thank anthologist Rick Klaw for *The Apes of Wrath*, a treasure trove of nineteen short stories about our simian cousins, from Poe's "The Murders in the Rue Morgue" to Kafka's "A Report to the Academy." Klaw's omnibus also includes "The Men in the Monkey Suit," Mark Finn's nonfiction tribute to those eccentrics who realized an actor could earn a decent living in Golden Age Hollywood if he constructed his own gorilla outfit, studied primate behavior at the San Diego Zoo, and routinely showed up at B-movie casting calls.

My beloved wife and indefatigable in-house editor, Kathryn Morrow, read multiple drafts of every *Behold the Ape* chapter and ornamented the margins with lapidary and incisive comments. I am most fortunate to have a collaborator who brings such passion and erudition to the intricacies of the comma and the mysteries of the cosmos.

ABOUT THE AUTHOR

Having arrived on the planet in 1947, James Morrow spent his adolescence in Hillside Cemetery, not far from his birthplace in Philadelphia, pursuing his passion for 8mm genre moviemaking. Before going off to college, he and his friends used their favorite graveyard location for a half-dozen fantasy and horror films, including adaptations of "The Rime of the Ancient Mariner" and "The Tell-Tale Heart."

After receiving a BA degree from the University of Pennsylvania and an MAT from the Harvard Graduate School of Education, Morrow spent a decade working for public school systems in Massachusetts, then began channeling his storytelling urge toward the creation of satiric novels. His acerbic assessment of the nuclear arms race, *This Is the Way the World Ends*, was the BBC's selection as best science-fiction novel of 1986. His next dark comedy, *Only Begotten Daughter*, chronicling the escapades of Jesus's divine half-sister in contemporary Atlantic City, won the World Fantasy Award.

Throughout the 1990s Morrow devoted his energies to killing God, an endeavor he pursued through three interconnected novels: *Towing Jehovah* (World Fantasy Award), *Blameless in Abaddon* (*New York Times* Notable Book), and *The Eternal Footman*. Having grown sick of his Creator, and vice-versa, the author next attempted to dramatize the birth of the scientific worldview. Critic Janet Maslin called *The Last Witchfinder* "an inventive feat." A thematic sequel, *The Philosopher's Apprentice*, was praised by NPR as "an ingenious riff on *Frankenstein*." Morrow's most recent irreverent epic, *Galápagos Regained* (Grand Prix de l'Imaginaire), narrates the adventures of Charles's Darwin's fictional zookeeper.

The author's stand-alone novellas includes *City of Truth* (Nebula Award), *Shambling Towards Hiroshima* (Theodore Sturgeon Memorial Award), *The Asylum of Dr. Caligari* (Shirley Jackson Award finalist), and *The Madonna and the Starship*. Morrow's work has been translated into thirteen languages. He lives in State College, Pennsylvania, with his wife Kathryn and three adopted dogs.

IF YOU LIKED ...

If you liked *Behold the Ape*, you might also enjoy:

Lost Among the Stars
by Paul Di Filippo

The Wandering Warriors
by Alan Smale and Rick Wilber

The Comet Chronicles
by Brian Herbert

Our list of other WordFire Press authors and titles is always growing. To find out more and to shop our selection of titles, visit us at:
wordfirepress.com

- facebook.com/WordfireIncWordfirePress
- twitter.com/WordFirePress
- instagram.com/WordFirePress
- bookbub.com/profile/4109784512

Printed in Dunstable, United Kingdom